tackling dad

elizabeth levy

HARPERCOLLINS*PUBLISHERS*

Library of Congress Cataloging-in-Publication Data
Levy, Elizabeth
Tackling Dad / Elizabeth Levy.— 1st ed.
    p.   cm.
Summary: When Cassie tries out for the middle school football team, she faces unex-
pected opposition from her father, an ex-professional football player.
    ISBN-10: 0-06-000051-1 — ISBN-10: 0-06-000050-3 (lib. bdg.)
    ISBN-13: 978-0-06-000051-6 — ISBN-13: 978-0-06-000050-9 (lib. bdg.)
    [1. Football—Fiction. 2. Fathers and daughters—Fiction. 3. Middle schools—Fiction.
4. Schools—Fiction.] I. Title.
PZ7.L5827Tac 2005   2004027657
[Fic]—dc22   CIP
                                                                                    AC
Typography by Sasha Illingworth
1 2 3 4 5 6 7 8 9 10
❖
First Edition

To my Father-
Elmer Irving Levy

special thanks

to Brant Spencer Amundson who shared his
knowledge and love of football and actually had
the patience to teach me how to put on my
pads. Thanks also to Harold Robinson who teaches
NFL drills at Chelsea Piers. Thanks to Amy Berkower
and Ruth Katcher for helping me get to
the end zone and to Tony Piccolo and Robie Harris
for being such wonderful sounding boards.
Thanks also to Bill Harris, the original Big Beef.
And special thanks to Dr. Murray List for
keeping Cassie and her family honest.

Contents

TRIPLE THREAT

"GO FOR IT!" SHOUTED OSCAR. IT WAS A HOT Saturday morning in early September. School had just started and we didn't have much homework yet. The smell of grass and dirt and pine trees in the Harrises' backyard made me want to stay there forever.

Oscar stood with his back to me and tossed a football over his head like a bride throwing a bouquet. I caught it and ran in his direction. He tried to tackle me, but I made a quick cut and got past him. He held his hands out, ready to grab me, but I veered right, then gave him a head-fake and ran right past him, all of him. Oscar's got about forty pounds on me. I'm five-foot-five, tall for my age, and I weigh 125, most of it muscle. Oscar is five-foot-seven and weighs 160. Just like me, he had a growth spurt when we moved from elementary school to middle school. In elementary school, he was the fat kid, and I always stuck up for him. Now we're both going into seventh grade. He's hefty, not fat, and he's even gotten pretty good-looking, at least that's what my friends say. It's hard to see that in someone you've known since day care. And played ball with.

Oscar didn't fall for my first head-fake, so I pivoted fast, taking one step back, and I spun to the left, putting on a burst of speed. I made it to the tree that was our end zone.

"TOUCHDOWN!" I shouted.

Oscar laughed. "Good one!" he shouted.

It wasn't real football. It was just a backyard game, but we loved it. We live in Clarence, New York, which is nestled right near Rich Stadium where the Buffalo Bills play pro ball. In our town, everyone has football in their blood, and I have the right bloodline. Dad was known as a triple threat, a running back who could run, throw, and tackle hard. And I inherited all his skills.

A few years ago, I was the star of our Peewee football team. Oscar's dad was our coach. When I was about seven, he told me that I had an innate sense for finding my way upfield. These were long words for a little kid, but I knew he was telling me I could be proud.

Even in the Peewee League, it's a big deal to be good. As a little kid, everybody looks up to you. You're talked about as being the next hero and idol. And I had it all. I was the kid with the fast feet and plenty of size. I was as big as anybody on the team. I was fearless.

Back then I thought being the superstar of our Peewee League was bigger than being Miss America. That was the catch. On our Peewee team, I was the only starter who could also someday qualify for Miss America.

I used to imagine myself running out in front of the huge crowds at Rich Stadium, where the Bills play, and hearing the announcer's voice boom, "And now, playing running back, western New York's born and bred, Clarence's own Cassie Fowler." My favorite daydream was that I was the one who saved the Bills. I was the running back who was so quick, so sure on her feet, that I brought back the glory. Then I went on to become the president of the United States, the first professional football player ever to do so.

Okay, I was only ten. I'm thirteen now. I know I'm not going to be Miss America *and* a pro football player, and I probably won't be president. I'm on our junior high track team. My football career came to a screeching halt two years ago when my dad got remarried. My dad quit coming to my games. I started winning races at school. Mom started talking to me about money, and telling me that track could be my ticket to a scholarship for college. I decided to concentrate on running.

My football skills still come in handy. Out on the track if anyone tries to push me around, I push back at them. Every fall, though, I miss football. Oscar and I still love tossing around the football together and playing scrimmage, just the two of us in his backyard.

Just then Oscar's dad came outside. Beef Harris is my dad's best friend. They played first string together in junior high and high school. Beef got his nickname in high school. He was a beefy guy, and he loved to eat meat. Then when he had a son, he named him Oscar after Oscar Mayer hot dogs. Our parents' generation has a lot to answer for in the name department.

Oscar is sometimes known as Little Beef. It was better

than Oscar the Wiener, his other nickname, but kids don't call him that when his dad's around.

"Hi, Uncle Beef," I said. Even though he's not my real uncle, our families are so close I've always called him Uncle Beef. It might be one of the funniest names in the world, but then he's one of the funniest men I've ever known—and the nicest.

"Hi, Cassie. You've still got the moves," he said. "You guys want to play two against one?"

Oscar laughed. "You think we can't get past you, Dad?" he hooted.

"Listen, son, just try it."

Oscar tossed the ball to his dad.

Uncle Beef made a big deal out of twirling the football in his hands. "You know, Cassie, your dad and I used to play backyard football all the time, just like you and Oscar. I can still see your dad trying to get past me. And lots of times he did head-fake, even though I was sure I had him. I can still see him with blood gushing from his nose when he caught my heel in his face. The little bump in his nose? That came from my shoe when we were both about your age. . . ."

"Dad, is this all going to be nostalgia, or are you going to throw the ball?" asked Oscar.

"Cassie, are you tired of my stories?"

"Well, Uncle Beef, I have heard how you broke Dad's nose about a hundred times."

Uncle Beef laughed. He stood with his back to us and tossed the ball over his head. Oscar and I scrambled for it, but I got it and Uncle Beef ran after me. I could feel his long arms grabbing me, but I pivoted, put my head down, and ran as fast as I could, my hands cradling the football in my belly, careful to protect it. Uncle Beef's big hands batted at the ball, but I held on. I could feel the hot adrenaline flowing through me. It gave me an extra burst of power, and again I made it around the pine tree, our end zone.

"Another touchdown for Cassie Fowler!" I yelled.

"She's beating us both, Oscar," said Uncle Beef. "You and the other girls ready for the Powderpuff game next Thursday?"

Powderpuff is played by girls—the seventh-grade girls against the eighth graders. Every year, during the second week of school, Coach Harris organizes a pep rally, and the Powderpuff game is the big attraction—especially because the boys dress as girl cheerleaders. I'm the captain of the seventh-grade Powderpuff team. Unfortunately, none of my friends were quite as enthusiastic about the big game.

I wished my friends liked to play as much as I did. But I knew they were just sort of humoring me. "I called a practice for tomorrow morning in the park," I told Uncle Beef, "but I'm not sure who will show up."

"We need a crowd," said Uncle Beef. "I need some new recruits. I've had trouble fielding a team lately because of competition from all the boys who have decided to play soccer and lacrosse. I never thought I'd see the day when the stands would be empty on a Thursday afternoon."

Last year, the middle school team had a losing record, 2-7. Uncle Beef hates losing, the way cats hate taking a bath. I remember that from playing for him. I'm a little like that too. I guess it takes one to know one.

Uncle Beef looked at his watch. "It's noon, Cassie. Won't your dad be picking you up at home?"

Uncle Beef knew my custody schedule as well as the football schedule, and it was just as regular. Every Saturday at noon, my dad picked me up. Every Sunday I came back home to Mom.

"If you want, you can invite him back here," suggested Uncle Beef. "We could have a little scrimmage, just the four of us. . . ."

"Maybe," I said doubtfully.

Uncle Beef nodded his head. He knew things were complicated.

I did too.

YOUR DAD'S HERE

I RAN BACK HOME. MOM LOOKED UP AT THE clock. "Your dad will be here any minute." He's always "your dad"—as if he's mine and had nothing to do with her.

"I was just playing football with Oscar and Uncle Beef."

"What else is new?" asked Mom, laughing. Uncle Beef and his wife, Robie, somehow had managed to stay friends with both my parents.

"I'll get washed," I said, looking at my grass-stained knees.

"Good," said Mom.

I went up to the bathroom. I didn't have time for a shower, so I just used a washcloth. I hadn't realized I had scraped both my knees. A thin layer of blood was mixed in with the grass stains. It didn't really hurt. I wiped it off and put on an antiseptic cream. Mom always kept plenty of it around.

"Cassie, your father's here," I heard my mom yell. She didn't use his name, Geoff. It's pronounced like the regular Jeff, but it's the Irish spelling, G-e-o-f-f-r-e-y.

I stood at the top of the stairs and looked down. Dad and

I both had more freckles on our faces than anybody could count. He hadn't bothered to take off his sunglasses in front of Mom. His glasses covered his blue eyes.

"Hi, sweetie," he said quietly. When I was younger, I didn't realize my father was handsome. I don't think most little kids do. Now that I'm almost thirteen, I see the way women and girls look at him—even my friends sometimes. They say his crooked nose makes him look even more hand-some, rugged. Dad is tall and still athletic, and he moves with grace and style.

"Hi, Dad," I said. I came down the steps quickly, gave him a kiss, and then stood at my mom's side. I was three inches taller than Mom and probably weighed fifteen pounds more than she did. Almost all of my weight was muscle. I hugged Mom good-bye, and she had to lift her chin to get it over my shoulder.

"Have a good weekend, sweetie," she said.

Both Mom and Dad call me sweetie, especially in front of each other, as if I'm a piece of candy that they don't want to share.

Sweetie is not my name. I'm Cassie, short for Cassandra. What a name to give a kid! I was in fourth grade when my teacher had us do a project on what our names mean. Imagine being nine years old and finding out you're named after a Greek demigoddess who had the gift of telling the future, except that it turned into a curse because nobody believed her.

I don't mind being named after a demigoddess. I like that word "demi"—half goddess, half human. I'm built a little too solidly for a goddess. In fact, I've got such big shoulders most people wouldn't guess that I'm good at track. I don't look fast. Before a track meet, Mom says that I look like I'm going to the guillotine. I've got a long face, and ever since fifth grade, when I grew four inches, my shoulders kind of slump.

But I've got the same speed that used to help me in football. My track coach says I'm one of the few runners she knows who can start at a flat-out sprint and then get faster! Even girls with a real kick at the end usually can't catch me.

I walked out onto the driveway with Dad. My five-foot-five height still brought me only to his broad shoulders. Dad is six-foot-two and weighs well over two hundred pounds. I dumped my backpack into the back of Dad's Honda. It hit the baby's car seat and ended up wedged on the floor.

Mom watched us from inside the house.

"Your mom looks good," Dad said.

"Yes, she does," I said. They almost never use each other's first names, Marie and Geoff. They're not hard names to remember. It's almost as if their saying "your mom" and "your father" is a way of trying to forget each other, but they can't because of me.

They've known each other forever. They were both born right here in Clarence. Mom and Dad and Uncle Beef and Robie all went to the same junior high where Oscar and I go, only now it's called a middle school. Mom and Dad started dating at the end of seventh grade, when they were thirteen. How weird is that? They moved on to become the high school football hunk and the brainy cheerleader who always got good grades. When they got married during their freshman year in college, they were so adorable that everyone just assumed they'd be together all their lives. Then they had me the year they graduated from college. I was cute with curly blond hair that got redder as I got older and sturdy little legs. Both sets of grandparents thought that I'd have lots of brothers and sisters who would fill up the house.

I wanted a baby brother or a baby sister too. But that didn't happen. I can still remember them sitting me down when I was nine and telling me that *Mom and Dad both would always love me, but that they couldn't live together.*

I hated that speech. I hated it then, and I still hate it. Even when I was nine, I could tell it sounded fake. It was. Serena was already in the picture. Both Mom and Dad knew, but they didn't think that I should. I found out quickly enough. Even Oscar knew about Serena before I did.

"Serena's waiting for us at home," said Dad. He glanced over at me. "You look a little sweaty."

"I was playing scrimmage with Oscar," I explained. "Uncle Beef asked if you wanted to go over there and toss the ball around."

"I think we'd better go home," said Dad. "Jason's been a handful lately."

When Serena and Dad got married two years ago, I was in their wedding. If the real Cassandra had been able to see the future, she would have laughed her head off over having me as a namesake. I never would have predicted I'd walk down the aisle in a puffy purple bridesmaid's dress at my father's wedding. I also would have never predicted that my baby brother would be a half brother—or a demi, like a demigoddess.

Dad turned to me. "What's new?" He yawned.

"Tired?" I asked.

"Jason was up last night. Poor Serena. I promised her we'd take Jason out so she can get some sleep."

"Sure, Dad," I said.

"Serena's a wreck today. . . ."

"I like playing with Jason," I said, and I meant it.

Let me tell you, if I ever have kids, I'm going to do a little research. Even with a different wife, Dad picked another Greek name, and there is nothing Greek about us. The original Jason was hated by both his father and his mother—not to mention his stepfather. As terrible as Greek myths are, it's comforting to realize that family dramas like ours were also happening four thousand years ago. Not that my life is as bad as the original Jason's or Cassandra's. As far as I know the ancient Greek gods and goddesses didn't play Powderpuff football.

Dad looked at me. "What are you grinning about?" he asked.

I giggled. "Just thinking about Greek mythology," I said, knowing that would impress him. "Imagining all those Greek goddesses playing football. By the way, speaking of goddesses, did you know I'm the seventh-grade Powderpuff captain? We're going to practice tomorrow. Want to come coach us? The game's on Thursday."

"I'll have to ask Serena," Dad said.

"Why do you need permission? You could bring Jason."

"I told you, I'll ask Serena," repeated Dad.

"Don't put yourself out. It's probably only the last time you'll ever get to see me play football."

"Is that sarcasm?" Dad wasn't laughing, and neither was I. "I like it better when I watch you run track," he added. "That's your sport."

"Well, you didn't make it to that many of my track meets," I muttered.

We pulled into Dad's driveway. He still lives in the Pinetree townhouse complex that he moved into when he moved out of our house three years ago. It's got two bedrooms. For the year that Dad lived there alone, and only dated Serena, it was just him and me on weekends. My bedroom was his den, and it was where the television was. Every Sunday we would watch football together, tossing the Nerf ball between us, trying not to get it into the guacamole or the Buffalo chicken wings. The wings are something good named after Buffalo, unlike the Buffalo Bills, who lost the Super Bowl four times.

When Dad first got divorced, he and I decorated my bedroom in his house as a tribute to the Buffalo Bills. The daybed held a herd of stuffed buffalos, and the walls were covered with autographed pictures of the team's stars.

Now my old bedroom is Jason's, and so are the herd of buffalos and the autographed pictures. I sleep on a foldout couch in the living room.

"Shh," Dad said as we walked in through the garage. "Jason's sleeping."

The house smelled of garlic and onions. Serena was in the kitchen.

"Hi, Cassie," she said, lifting her head. She had black hair so straight and flat that it covered her head like a helmet, and dark, almond-shaped eyes. At least Serena didn't call me sweetie. "I'm making the spaghetti sauce that you like for dinner tonight."

I walked over and gave her a hug. "Oh, good," I said. It was not that I love Serena's sauce so much. It is just that it is so much better than the other things Serena cooks, like the tofu burgers and couscous specialties.

Serena was a vegetarian and had turned my father into one too. The weekend trips to McDonald's when Dad was a bachelor were out, now. The first year after Mom and Dad separated, Dad stopped drinking. Gradually he began to cut out all meat and sweets. Dad tried to explain to me that sometimes when people stopped one bad habit they had to stop all of them. He claims that once he stopped drinking, his taste buds changed, and beef didn't taste good to him anymore.

Dad was never a falling-down drunk. But most nights, Mom would join him for one beer, but then Dad would have another and another. The more he drank, the quieter he became. The thing is, now that he's sober, he's still pretty quiet.

My vegetarian friends all think it is really cool that a big ex-football player like my dad is a vegetarian. Even my non-vegetarian friends think that Dad's being a recovered alcoholic is great—as if that cured everything. But I miss the barbecues that Mom and Dad used to have with their friends. I don't miss the drinking, but I miss the laughing.

I went to the refrigerator to browse.

"Looking for something?" Serena asked. I took a deep

breath. I didn't hate Serena, but she makes me feel like a guest in a place where I used to feel at home.

I took out a carrot and went to sit on a cane chair by the counter. There was a bunch of parsley sitting on the blue countertop. Sunshine was drifting in through the kitchen window.

"You can cut the parsley for me," said Serena. "That would be helpful."

I took out a knife from the block and started to quickly chop the parsley. Green bits of leaves flew from the edge of the knife.

"Careful," warned Dad. He watched me nervously.

"I'm fine," I said, letting the parsley fly.

"Cassie's playing Powderpuff football," Dad told Serena.

Serena stared at me. "That sounds cute! You know, Cassie, I'd be happy to give you some tips about makeup. You've got such pretty eyes, and a little blusher on your cheeks would be nice. You're not too young."

I laughed. "Serena, it's not that kind of powderpuff. It's a real football game."

"Well, not exactly real," said Dad.

"It's played with a real football," I explained to Serena, ignoring Dad. "It's a game the girls play at a pep rally before the boys' football season tryouts."

"What do you wear?" asked Serena. When Serena first met me, I think she had fantasies that she would get a stepdaughter who would love a makeover and adore shopping. The problem is that I am one of the few thirteen-year-old girls in America who hate to shop. Serena is as petite as my mom. Why does a guy as big as my dad choose pixie-looking women? I chopped harder.

"You know," said Serena, "you don't always have to wear those big shirts. There are a lot of styles that would look good on you."

I continued chopping the parsley and didn't look up.

"Whoa there, little girl," said Dad. "You don't have to murder the parsley."

I looked up at him and chopped even faster. I no longer liked being called "little girl."

Dad didn't tell me to slow down again.

And I didn't.

I just kept chopping.

Dad stood over me. He looked down at the Band-Aid on my knee.

"What did you do to yourself?" he asked.

"Just scraped it playing football this morning with Oscar."

"Isn't Oscar a little big for you to handle?"

"I can get past him just fine," I bragged. "I still have the moves."

"Well, just be careful he doesn't fall on you. He must have fifty pounds on you."

"He's not fat," I argued.

"I didn't say he was, sweetheart," said Dad.

Dad always called me sweetheart when he was trying to avoid a fight.

WHO WANTS TO BE A STAR?

JASON WOKE ME UP SUNDAY MORNING. HE WAS dressed in a diaper and his Buffalo Bills T-shirt. He climbed up onto the sofa bed. I kissed him and blew another kiss onto his stomach. He laughed and I did too. When he laughs, he throws his arms wide open.

Before he was born, Dad and Serena sat me down and told me that they'd understand if I had conflicted feelings about a stepbrother. They needn't have bothered. I have lots of conflicting feelings, but not about Jason.

Serena and Dad expected me to explode with sibling rivalry. Even Mom told me I should expect it to be difficult to have a baby stepbrother. But Jason himself is a hoot. I even like changing diapers. I'm good at it. It's a little like origami. It's quick. There's a mess . . . and then it's gone. It isn't like the rest of my life, where messes tend to stick around.

I changed Jason and brought him into the kitchen. Serena and Dad were fixing breakfast.

"Do you two want to bring Jason to the park this

morning?" I asked. "I'm meeting Molly and Ella and some other girls to practice for Powderpuff."

"So is Powderpuff a real game?" Serena asked. "I've never heard of girls playing football." Sometimes I forget that Serena isn't from around here. She moved here from New York City, and she met Dad at Alcoholics Anonymous.

"It's a game where girls play football. It's at a pep rally. It's fun," I explained.

"Geoff, take Jason. Go with Cassie," said Serena. "I could use a little quiet time after breakfast."

As we left the house, Dad pushed Jason in his stroller. Dad and I didn't talk too much. My father and I have never chatted the way Mom and I do. He's just a quieter person. Actually, I've always liked the times when we don't talk. It's when we do talk that we get in trouble.

When we got to the park, the other girls weren't there yet. I took the football out of my backpack. A football is harder and tougher-looking than any other ball. It's not as easy to throw as a round ball, but once you learn how, it spirals fast and true.

I patted the ball twice and then put my fingers over the laces toward the back. I threw it hard into Dad's hands. Jason watched us from his stroller. Dad caught the ball, but he had to take a step backward. I think he was surprised that I could throw it hard enough to make his hands sting.

I looked up and saw Eric Spencer and Oscar walking toward us.

"Hey, nice throw!" Eric shouted. I grinned.

"Yeah, we're going to teach you guys how to do it," I said.

Eric was a year ahead of me, in eighth grade. He played varsity football, and we had played together in Peewee. We were both running backs, and we both played hard.

"Hi, Uncle Geoff," said Oscar. "It's cool to see you playing football with Cassie. Cassie and I were playing yesterday. She's still pretty good."

"Yeah, I know," said Dad. "She just stung my hands with a throw. Somehow I never pictured Cassie as a Powderpuff."

"She's not," said Oscar.

"Thank you, Oscar," I said. I curtsied to him. He blushed, so I punched him lightly on the arm.

Eric made a face. "Come on, Osc," he said.

"Where are you going?" I asked him.

"We're going to lift weights at the Y," said Eric. "We're meeting Brant and Harold. We've got tryouts coming up next week."

"Brings back memories," said Dad.

"You look fit enough to play," said Eric, admiringly. "You still lift, don't you? I've seen you at the Y."

"I do it when I can fit it in," said Dad. I could tell that he liked the flattery. "So, Oscar, you going to dress up like a cheerleader for the Powderpuff game? That's what your dad and I used to do."

Oscar looked embarrassed. "Yeah, we still do that," he said.

"Can't wait to see you in a skirt," I teased.

"I'll never forget your dad, jiggling out on the field," said Dad.

"I have Dad's outfit," said Oscar. "Mom kept it. Do you have yours, Uncle Geoff?"

"No, it went out with the trash. To tell the truth, I'm surprised that Beef still puts on the Powderpuff game."

"It *is* a little silly," said Eric.

Just then, my two best friends, Ella and Molly, showed up. Oscar looked nervous. He always seemed to get nervous around Ella.

Ella and Molly ignored us and made a beeline for Jason. Jason is a magnet for my friends. They love to coo over him. I have to admit that with his curly hair and chubby cheeks, he is mighty cute.

"Hi, Geoffrey," Ella said to my father. "Jason looks so big." Ella has been calling my father by his first name all her life. Of all of my friends, Ella is the one who looks most like a teen model. She is as thin as a reed with long legs. She looks more like a sprinter than I do because I've started to get broad on top. Ella used to be a gymnast, and lately she's taken up rock climbing. She can climb the rock wall at school like a spider.

"Hi, Mr. Fowler," said Molly. Molly is much more shy than either Ella or me, but on the track, she can be fierce. She hates to lose, and she hates to have anyone pass her, especially me. Both Molly and Ella have grit. I think it's why we like one another so much.

"Oscar was just telling us about his cheerleading outfit," I teased him. "He's wearing his dad's."

Oscar looked down at his big belly. "Don't expect too much," he said.

"Come on, Wiener," said Eric, using the nickname that Oscar hated the most.

"I'd better be going too. I need to take Jason home," said Dad. "I'll walk you guys out of the park. See you later, sweetie. I'll meet you back at the house."

Jason grinned at me. He didn't look like a kid who needed to go home. He looked wide awake and he wasn't fussing. I knew Dad didn't have to get back. Even on our one day a week together, he'd rather be with Serena.

"See you later," I said. I turned my back on him and flipped the ball to Molly. It spiraled through the air and bounced off her hands. "Ouch!" she shouted. "I forgot how hard a football is." She picked it up off the grass. "This thing isn't even shaped like a ball. It looks like a missile. No wonder boys like to play with it so much."

"Right—and there's no violence or bumping in track and field," I said.

Molly grinned. She patted the ball. "I remember once in a Peewee game, you pretended to hand the ball off to me. You got creamed, but you still managed to get down the field and score a touchdown. Your dad went crazy."

"Well, he had a head start in those days," I reminded her.

"He never acted drunk," said Ella. "I think it's so cool that he did something with his life and admitted his mistakes. Is he coming to see you play Powderpuff?"

"If he gets permission from Serena." I shrugged my shoulders. "Anyhow, it doesn't matter. What matters is that we have the best Powderpuff game on Thursday! Agreed?"

"Agreed!" shouted Molly. She threw the football. It teetered in the air. "I forgot how hard it is to throw a tight spiral," she said.

"It comes back," I said. I threw a perfect one to her, my fingers cocking around the ball. "When you've done it a million times, it becomes second nature."

Molly threw the ball to Ella, and Ella flipped it to me. I tucked it under my armpit. Ella put out her hands to tag me, but I did a spin move on her and drove down the field.

"Ahh . . . the moves come back," I shouted.

By now the other seventh-grade girls who had promised to play had shown up, and I taught them some simple plays. After about an hour, most of the girls were pretty tired.

Ella said, "That's enough." Everybody agreed with her. I looked at my watch with its peacock band, a present from Serena, who was always hoping that I would dress more femininely. It was still early.

"What's the matter?" I asked. "We still have a lot of stuff we could do."

Ella rolled her eyes at me. "It's a Powderpuff game, Cassie. Get it through your head that it is not a big deal."

"Don't you want to play?" I asked her.

She shrugged. "Yeah, I'll play. I promised you I would. But everybody just comes to see the guys wear fake boobs in their cheerleading outfits. That's all anyone pays attention to at these things."

I knew she was right, but it didn't make it any easier that she was using practically the same words as my dad. Powderpuff was just a joke.

Molly put her arm around me as we packed up. "It'll be fun," she said. "But afterward it'll be time to put away your football toys."

"I put him away long ago," I said.

Molly cocked an eyebrow at me.

"What?" I demanded.

"You said 'put him away,' as if football were a guy," Molly pointed out.

"Just a slip of the tongue," I said quickly.

Ella looked at me. "Tell the truth. If you could play only one sport and it was totally your choice, it would be football. You'd have Coach Harris as your coach, right?"

I was the only one who ever called Coach Harris Uncle Beef. "Don't be silly," I said, perhaps a little too quickly. "Remember the drills he used to have us run in Peewee? Who wants to go through that again?"

Ella laughed. "You do. Look how psyched you are about the Powderpuff game. You won't be satisfied unless you put on a show, like at the track."

"I'm not a showy runner," I said.

"Yeah, right," said Ella. "You're not showy. You never shoot out of the blocks, but just let somebody try to pass you, and you're all elbows."

"I don't push first. I just don't like it if somebody crowds me, so I fight back."

"Look, Cassie," said Ella. "This isn't a criticism. I love having you on my team. I know you're going to do anything to win."

"Not at any cost. I'm not one of those kids."

Ella and Molly looked at me.

"I'm not!" I argued.

"I thought we'd *all* have fun at the Powderpuff game," I

said. I was smarting from the idea that my friends thought I fought too hard to win.

"We will," said Ella. "We'll get to see Eric Spencer and Brant Amudsen in short skirts. Not to mention Oscar. He'll be worth the price of admission. I bet he looks cute." It surprised me that Ella would single out Oscar for cuteness.

"Maybe we can have a contest for the cutest boy in a girl's cheerleading outfit," said Molly.

"Eric would win hands down!" I blurted out. "He's tall, dark, and perfectly shaped for a running back, with wide shoulders and slim hips."

Molly collapsed into giggles. "Slim hips! Wide shoulders! It sounds like somebody's got a crush!"

"No, I don't," I protested.

"He's so conceited," said Ella.

I licked my lips nervously. Molly caught my eye.

"Cassie likes guys who are cocky," teased Molly.

"Why is it cocky if you're really good at something?" I argued.

"See? We hit a nerve," teased Ella.

"But he *is* really good," I said. "Everybody talks about him as if he's got a big fat ego. People think that I'm cocky on the track. You even said it about me, but when I run a race, I gotta believe that I've worked harder than the other team and that I can beat them. Does that make me cocky? What's the difference between believing in yourself and being cocky?"

"Are we talking about you or Eric now?" asked Molly.

I shrugged. I really wasn't sure.

THE BIG 55

ON THURSDAY MORNING, I WOKE UP TO THE sound of rain drumming on my window. I looked outside. The sky was so gray and foggy that I couldn't even see the garage door.

I went into the bottom drawer of my dresser and pulled out Dad's jersey, which I believe was the only piece of his clothing still in the house. It was shredded at the elbow, but I didn't care. It had the number 55 on the back. All through junior high, high school, and college, he always wore the number 55.

Hand Jive Five was his nickname because he had so many groovy moves. My birthday is May 5—5/5. When I was born on May 5, he took it as a sign of some sort. He used to tell me that he knew he was destined to be close to his daughter. I'm not sure that Dad and destiny ever got together on that one. If they had, I don't think he would have left home.

I tucked his shirt into my long blue shorts with the Buffalo Bills logo. We're allowed to wear shorts that go to our knees to school until the middle of September. All the girls on the Powderpuff team had to wear blue and white, our school's colors—and of course the colors of the Buffalo Bills. We were very proud of the fact that we were the only middle school in our division that got to wear blue and white.

Mom was sipping coffee when I went into the kitchen. She looked up and saw me in my father's shirt. "You're wearing number 55," she said.

"Five is my lucky number," I reminded her.

Mom smiled. She poured me some orange juice and stared out the window. "Do you think this rain will be over before the end of your school day?" she asked. "If it isn't, won't they call off the game?" she asked.

"Mom, it's football. We play in the rain." I didn't tell her that she sounded like Serena.

Mom sighed. "Ah, standing in the rain on the sidelines on a Thursday afternoon. What a treat!"

"You don't have to go," I told her.

"Nonsense. I'll be there to cheer you on this afternoon. Have I ever missed any of your games or meets unless I really had to?"

Her question needed no answer. Mom did go to almost all my track meets. However, I knew what she was really asking me: *Didn't you notice that I rearranged my work schedule so that I could go to all of your meets, but your dad couldn't be bothered? Haven't I been the better parent?* Children of divorced families get to be fluent in a language we wish we never had to learn.

"I think Dad's coming to the Powderpuff game," I said to her.

Now the rain was coming down even harder. "It's going to be very muddy," she said.

"I don't mind mud," I said. "You know what happens when there's mud on the field?"

"I get back a muddy daughter?" Mom teased.

"Well, yes," I said. "But it also means that we have to do a lot of running, not passing. Who's the best runner? Me!"

Mom laughed. "What I like about you is that you don't lack confidence."

"Should I?" I asked. I remembered what people said about Eric behind his back.

"No, sweetie. It's one of the things that make me proud of you."

She glanced down at my dad's shirt and then hugged me tight.

I put on my slicker and waited for the bus. When we got to Molly's stop, she dived into the bus, her ponytail drenched. "If this doesn't let up, will they call off the game?"

I stared at her. "You sound like my mother. Football's not like baseball. Football players aren't afraid of rain." I opened my slicker and showed her my shirt.

"You're already dressed for the game?"

"It's a pep rally," I said. "I've got pep."

All morning when I looked out the window, I could see the rain coming down. I was relieved when, after lunch, Coach Harris got on the loudspeaker. "Everybody, remember to come to the field for our Powderpuff pep rally. Rain means good luck in some cultures. So let's see a good crowd out there to support our team. And speaking of the team, anybody who's thinking of joining the football team, remember we've got tryouts on Monday. See you all out there."

After school, I joined all the girls in our locker room. I, of course, had been dressed for the game all day. The eighth-grade team was captained by Miranda Kirby. Miranda, Molly, and I are all on the track team together. She does the high jump, and she's got even longer legs than Ella. She's tough. She can fall into the pit, clunk her head on the bar, and then get up and make the next jump as if nothing happened.

Miranda shook her head. "I don't mind a track meet in the rain, but this is ridiculous."

"Don't you want to play?" I asked her nervously.

"Well, I like the idea of kicking the butts of you seventh graders," said Miranda.

"We'll see who kicks butt," I warned her.

Miranda snorted.

I knew she thought her team wouldn't have any trouble burying us. She was in for a surprise.

We ran out onto the field. There wasn't much of a crowd. I scanned the parking lot for Dad's Honda, but I didn't see it. But my mother was there. She was standing on the sidelines in a huge blue slicker with CLARENCE COYOTES spelled out on the back in black. She'd had it since high school. I ran up to her. "Glad you're here," I shouted over the rain.

Uncle Beef waved her over to him. "Hey, Marie!" he shouted. "You're a die-hard fan." He opened up his big arms, gave her a huge hug, and kept his arm around her shoulders, as if to protect her from the rain.

"Are you really holding a pep rally in this weather?" Mom asked.

"The girls are here. The boys are getting changed."

"Getting changed?" Mom asked.

"Tradition," joked Uncle Beef. "Don't you remember seeing Geoff and me dressed like cheerleaders?"

"You never looked so cute," Mom teased him.

The girls called me to the middle of the field where they had started to warm up. The ground was already really sloppy, so we kept things simple, just doing easy stretches standing up so we didn't have to lie down in the mud.

Suddenly Ella whistled with her fingers to her teeth. The boys came running out of the locker room single file. Eric was the first one out. He was wearing a white sweater with fake boobs and a blue pleated cheerleader's skirt. He had on a curly blond wig. He had put on bright pink lip gloss that exaggerated his pouty lips. He waved as if he were the prettiest girl in the world and there was nothing to be embarrassed about. That was so like Eric. If he was going to look like a girl, he would be a pretty one.

Brant came out next. He had longish black hair, and he had put on some makeup, but he wore a sleeveless tank top, with no fake boobs. His big biceps made it clear that even if he was wearing a skirt, he was all boy.

The last one out was Oscar. Oscar looked anything but great. His belly hung out from the little pleated skirt he was wearing, and he waved his pom-poms.

"How did they find a skirt to fit him?" Molly giggled.

"It's his dad's outfit," I told her.

"I don't believe it," said Molly. "Coach Harris wore that?"

"I bet he looked as cute as Oscar," I said.

Oscar came running by. "Go, Oscar! Go, Oscar!" I shouted. Oscar blushed. He shook his pom-poms in my face and grinned.

Wet from the rain, the pom-poms soaked my face and jersey.

Oscar grinned at me shyly. "Go, Cassie! Go, girls!" he shouted, shaking his pom-poms and his bottom.

"Oscar, my boy, I don't think pleats suit you." I heard my father's voice before I saw him. "You're the spitting image of your dad in drag."

Eric stopped his prancing. He looked at Oscar a little jealously.

Uncle Beef came over and put his arm around my father. "Geoff, glad you've come to see Cassie play."

Mom nodded to Dad. She stepped away from Uncle Beef, but landed in a puddle.

Dad was staring at me. "You're wearing 55," Dad said.

"It's a lucky number," I said to him.

"Do you really think you need luck for a Powderpuff rally?" Dad asked. With anyone else, I would have thought he was being sarcastic. But Dad genuinely believes that if you don't know something, you should ask.

"No, Dad," I answered him seriously. "I don't need luck. I've got skill."

"Yes, you do on the track. But why go out on a sloppy field and risk injury if you don't have to?" He didn't wait for me to answer him. He turned to Uncle Beef, the only man around who was his size. The other fathers all looked small compared with the two of them.

"Seriously, Beef, are you really going to hold this game?"

"Why not? Your daughter won't melt in the rain. That sugar and spice stuff went out years ago."

"I'm not worrying about her melting, but there's no pep here. There's not really a crowd to rally."

At six-foot-four, Uncle Beef is the only man I know who can look down at Dad.

"The girls are here. They're ready to play. My boy is dressed like a cheerleader, and so are his friends."

"And a cute one at that," I added.

Molly and Ella both giggled. Eric took a step forward. "Look, if you're going to give prizes to who's the best-looking cheerleader here . . . I don't want to brag . . ."

"But you are bragging," teased Ella. "Honey, that shade of pink is so last year."

Eric didn't flinch. "Ella," he said, "I'm willing to let you paint my toenails if you want."

"Back off, big boy," said Ella. "I've got a game to play." She was laughing so hard she snorted.

"That's enough about the cheerleaders," said Coach Harris. "Let's get to the game." He blew his whistle and called all the seventh- and eighth-grade girls who were playing around him. "Okay, girls. This isn't tackle football. No rough stuff out there. That's not what this game is about. Miranda, you're the captain of the eighth graders. Cassie, you're the captain of the seventh. A coin flip will decide who gets the ball first. Cassie, you call it."

"Tails," Molly whispered in my ear. "It's lucky."

"Tails!" I shouted. The coin fell on the wet grass. It came up tails.

"We'll receive!" I shouted. I wanted to get my hands on the ball first. I shook hands with Miranda.

Coach Harris blew his whistle and the game began. Miranda kicked the ball right to me. I grabbed it and started running forward. The grass was so wet, my feet slipped out from under me, and I fell on my face. Mud streaked down my nose and cheeks. I wiped it off. I was mad. I was the team captain and I'd messed up already, but I wasn't going to do it again.

"Okay," I shouted. "One mistake doesn't mean it's over. Let's go!"

On the next play Ella slipped and fell forward into the mud. When she got up, she looked as if she had poured chocolate syrup all over herself.

"Are you sure this is supposed to be fun?" she sputtered.

"Yes!" I shouted. "Next play!"

"Is that our mud-wrestling play?" asked Amanda, one of the other girls on our team.

"The boys will like that," said Wilhelmina.

As if on cue, we heard the boys shouting, "Two, four, six, thud! Let's go, girls—you look good in mud!"

My entire team started laughing. I glared at them. "Come on, girls! We're not doing this for the boys! We're doing it for us!"

"Uh, Cassie?" Molly reminded me as we broke out of the

huddle. "We *are* doing this for the boys. It's just a pep rally."

Molly handed me the ball. I planted my right foot and moved my head to the left. The defender fell for my head-fake, the same move I had made on Oscar. My back foot slipped in the mud, forcing my legs into a split. I fell forward onto my face. Coach Harris blew his whistle. The play was dead. Nobody had tackled me, and we had lost yardage.

"Hey, Cassie!" shouted Eric. "You're supposed to wait till a defender gets to you before you fall down!"

I picked myself up, pulling a clump of mud out of my hair. I glared at him. I knew what I was doing! I didn't need his advice. Football was in my blood—my bones.

The game was supposed to last only an hour. But just fifteen minutes into it, it was clear that neither team was getting anywhere. We finally got close enough to the end zone so that Molly could boot the ball right through the goal-posts. We scored! But then the eighth graders came right back at us. From the ten-yard line, they scored a field goal too.

I went into the backfield to receive. It began to rain even harder. I looked up at the sidelines. Almost everybody who didn't have to be there had left. There were my mom and dad, standing under separate umbrellas, six feet apart.

Coach Harris blew his whistle. He brought both teams together. "Girls, I know you're playing your hearts out here, but I don't want to see anyone get hurt. We haven't seen any lightning, but I think it's time to call it a day."

"Give us time for one more play," I begged him.

"If the seventh graders can take it, we can," said Miranda.

Her shorts and T-shirt were caked with mud.

"Cassie's our captain," said Ella. "We stick together through mud or more mud."

"Remember, this was supposed to be a fun day," said Coach Harris.

The boys were under the stands, shivering, still dressed in their cheerleading outfits. They looked not just silly but cold too. The eighth-grade girls kicked off. The ball didn't come anywhere near me. Luckily Molly managed to fall on it. We were still a long way from the goal line.

We went into a huddle. "Come on, girls," I tried to rally my troops. "If we don't get one successful play off today in front of the boys, they'll never let us forget it."

We tried a fake. Ella folded her arms around her belly trying to look for all the world as if she had the ball hidden there. Miranda went after her.

I headed for the spot where I knew Molly's pass was coming. The ball wobbled, but I reached up and grabbed it, cradling it. My feet started churning from the moment I felt the ball in my fingers. One of the eighth graders tried to grab me. I spun away from her. There was nothing between me and the goalposts. Nothing, except Miranda. Somehow she had backpedaled in the mud. She held her hands wide, trying to tag me.

I tried to cut to my left, but my foot slipped in the mud. Still I managed to hold on to the football and remain upright. I tried to go forward, but with the wet mud, it was hard to get any forward momentum. Miranda was reaching out, ready to grab me.

I pushed her away with a stiff arm and charged into the end zone. Miranda slipped in the mud and fell on her rear. I couldn't believe it. I had scored. Molly and Ella were running to me, their arms wide open. We fell into the mud and laughed. We didn't care how dirty we were. We had won.

5

LOVING TO WIN, HATING TO LOSE

DAD AND MOM WERE BOTH CHEERING. I THREW my arms up and gave them a huge wave. All the girls piled on me as we celebrated. "Awesome!" shouted Ella. "Can we go home now?"

I nodded happily. Then I saw Miranda yelling at Coach Harris. He blew the whistle and signaled us to come back.

"No touchdown!" he said, waving his hand. "Cassie, that was a foul. You can't push Miranda down. Girls, that's it. The game ends in a tie. "

I glared at Uncle Beef, my hands on my hips.

Uncle Beef looked at me. "Don't look mad at me. You know the rules."

"I know." I sighed. Uncle Beef put his arm around me.

"Truth to tell, Cassie," he said, "I liked watching you play like that."

When I got to the sideline, my mom tried to hold an umbrella over me, as if I weren't already soaked through.

Dad stood to the side. He handed me a towel. "Thanks," I muttered.

"In that last run, you were almost home free," said Dad.

"*Almost* doesn't cut it," I said. "When Miranda fell because I straight-armed her, it was a foul. The touchdown didn't count."

"Well, a tie is not a win," said Mom. "But it's better than losing. And this way nobody lost."

My father caught my eye. "Look at Cassie's face. Nobody won! A tie is like kissing your brother or sister."

Mom laughed nervously. "That's ridiculous. Kissing your brother is very nice."

"Yeah, but not as nice as kissing someone who is cute!" said Dad. "Besides, this isn't about kissing!"

"Why are you raising your voice at me?" shouted my mother.

They glared at each other. I couldn't believe my parents were arguing in public about kissing

Mom looked at me, expecting that I would support her. Usually I don't agree with my father. I think Mom counts on that. But this time he was right. I hated having to settle for a tie.

"Let's go, Cassie," Mom said.

"I'll drive her home," said Dad. "My car's a mess anyhow."

"I'm here," said Mom. "She can go home with me."

"Really," I said. "It doesn't matter who gets the muddy daughter. Mom, you just had your car cleaned. Why doesn't Dad drive me home?"

"Fine," snapped Mom. I sighed.

I knew I had hurt her feelings. I hated that every little thing, such as who was going to drive me home, became a major deal.

"Dad, never mind," I said. "Mom can take me. Then you can go straight home to Serena and Jason."

I've learned to speak the hidden language too. Mom went to get her car. Dad was biting his lip. Now, his feelings were hurt. Yet he had only come to the game because I had shamed him into it. I gathered up my stuff. Dad turned away from me. I thought he was going home, but he ended up in the middle of the field talking to Eric.

Oscar came up to me. His cheerleader outfit looked soggy and pathetic. "Awful conditions," he said. "But your last run was the best. Especially when you almost ran over Miranda. That was cool."

"No, it wasn't. It cost us the game."

"Ties feel crummy," said Oscar.

I laughed.

"What did I say that was funny?" Oscar asked.

"Nothing," I said. "It's just that my dad said a tie was like kissing your brother or sister, and my mom almost snapped his head off."

"That's what my dad always says," said Oscar.

"What do I always say?" asked Uncle Beef.

"That a tie is like kissing your sister," said Oscar.

"You're right—I do say that," admitted Uncle Beef. "Ties don't feel great. But it usually is a sign that both teams played their hearts out. Cassie, I loved the way you made that run for daylight. If you can't fake out the defenders, you try to run over whatever's in your way. Kind of reminds me of your dad."

I drank in the praise.

"Thanks, Coach Harris," I said. "But I never should have shoved Miranda."

"Call me Uncle Beef now that the game's over," he said. "Cassie, I miss coaching you. There's no reason why you shouldn't be playing in a game where you can shove aside the defender."

"In track and field we have our share of bumps and elbows, but if you do too much it's a penalty," I said.

"You don't have track and field until the late winter and spring, right?" asked Uncle Beef.

"Right," I said.

"And, if I remember, soccer never really was your sport."

"It isn't," I said. "In the fall I just do weight training for track."

"Weight training's good for what I have in mind. Suppose you played for my team?"

"You want me to carry water for Oscar and Eric and the guys? Don't you have an equipment manager?"

"Actually, he graduated," said Uncle Beef. "But Ben Piccolo offered to take over. Everybody knows that last year we had a losing season. And we've got an even younger team this year. I'd like you to think about playing football again. Come on, Cassie. I know you. I saw the way you prepared for this game. You love to win. There's nothing like winning at football."

I loved winning our Peewee games. In football, you play any trick to win, not dirty tricks, but just using your mind and body to psych out your opponents. There's a lot more strategy in football than people realize.

Brute strength doesn't always win. In football, you're always trying to trick the other team. I do that even in track. When I'm running a race, if I know somebody ahead of me is struggling, even if I'm struggling too, when I pass them I pretend that it's easy. I always try to look like I've got so much gas left in the tank that passing them is a piece of cake. And it feels great!

Molly and Ella came running over to say good-bye. They looked like drowned rats, even though the rain had begun to lighten up. "We're going home," Ella said. "My mom's here. She's taking Molly. Are you going with one of your folks?"

I nodded.

Coach Harris looked thoughtful. "Girls," he said. "I was just talking to Cassie about trying out for football this year. What about you two?"

Molly and Ella stared at him. Coach Harris grinned. "I could use the three of you on my team. You work well together, and that's not something that can be taught easily. You three played like a team."

"Not for me, thank you," said Ella. "I'll be a cheerleader, though. Miranda talked me into going out for the cheerleading squad. She's the captain."

"What about you, Molly?" asked Coach Harris. "You kicked a mighty field goal in the rain and wind."

"Do you want me so you can get Cassie?" asked Molly.

Uncle Beef gave Molly his best smile, and believe me, he's got a great smile. "I need a good kicker. We don't have one." Just then there was a honk. My mother's car had turned up on the sideline.

Uncle Beef saw Dad in the middle of the field. "I'll go talk to your dad," he said.

I was so excited I could hardly stand still. Molly and Ella put their arms around me. "What do you think of what Uncle Beef said?" I whispered. "I mean, do you think it's silly?" There were no adults in earshot, no boys. It was just us, and I really wanted to know what they thought.

"You want to play so bad," teased Ella.

"But what about you, Molly?" I asked. "Would you play too?"

"The uniforms are cute!" whispered Molly. "We'd certainly be unusual."

"Molly," I asked, "are you serious? Would you really try out with me?"

"Sure," said Molly. We grinned at each other. She looked up and held out her hand. "It's even stopped raining. It's a sign."

I WENT TO BED SMILING

WHEN WE GOT TO THE SIDELINE, UNCLE BEEF HAD his arm around Dad. Earlier, he had wrapped his big arm around Mom, and now Dad. What planet did Uncle Beef come from? He walked Dad over toward Mom's car.

Uncle Beef grinned at me. "I was telling your dad, the more I think about it, the more I agree with myself. I know of other middle schools in our area where girls are playing football. In fact, some girls are playing in high school and college, for heaven's sake. There's even a pro women's league. They play tackle football in full gear."

My father stared at his best friend. "I told you, Beef. It's ridiculous."

"Welcome to the twenty-first century, my friend," said Uncle Beef. "As I just said, girls are playing football all over the country. Not many, I admit, but some, especially in middle school. And Molly and Cassie are about the same size as most of my players, except for Oscar. I remember coaching Cassie in Peewee. She's always been good. She's got speed and guts. Eric is good, but I need more than one back."

Mom rolled down her window. "Cassie, are you coming?"

"Just a minute, Marie," said Uncle Beef. "I was just talking to Geoff and Cassie. I want Cassie to try out for my football team on Monday. Molly, too. I'll call her parents tonight."

Mom shook her head. "That sounds way too dangerous, Beef."

Dad nodded. Great. Finally something my parents could agree on—my *not* playing football.

I had to speak up. "Mom, I could get hurt running track too! Remember when I pulled my hamstring? I love football. It could be so much fun to play again."

"Girls don't belong on the football field. She can't play," said Dad flatly.

Uncle Beef took a deep breath. "Why don't we let Cassie think about it over the weekend? Cassie, tryouts are on Monday. I am serious about wanting you on the team. And, Geoff, Marie, give her a chance to decide for herself."

Dad glared at him.

"I mean it," Uncle Beef said. He whispered something to Dad and then took off. Dad held open the door to Mom's car for me. Mom spread a towel on the seat. Dad helped her straighten it out. It was nice to think they could do some things together—even just keeping me from dripping all over Mom's car.

"You really got soaked," Dad said.

"I had fun," I reminded him.

"Beef is right," he said. "You did look good out there, but don't take him seriously about playing."

"Now that's a mixed message to give her," said Mom

quickly. Dad's head snapped back as if he had been slapped.

"What do you mean?" he asked.

"You tell her she can play, but not to take it seriously?"

"Do you want her to play football?"

"Of course not," snapped Mom.

"Can we please go home?" I said. "I'm muddy and cold."

"Sorry," Dad mumbled.

I glanced at Mom. I didn't want her telling Dad off. I just wanted to get out of there before they started fighting.

"It's okay, Dad," I said.

Mom put the car in gear. Dad shut the door. He waved at us as we left. That was the first time that I realized that he was wet too. He had taken the time to stand in the rain and listen to Uncle Beef. And then he had gone home alone.

"You must be exhausted," Mom said

"No," I said. I picked the caked mud off my knee. Underneath was a little sheen of blood. I hadn't even realized that I had scraped my knee in the same place I had hurt it playing with Oscar.

"You look tired," said Mom. "You were in the rain the whole time."

"The rain is fun," I snapped. "It fools the defenders."

"Cassie, what are you angry about?" Mom demanded. "Was it something your dad said?"

I wondered if she knew how many times she asked that question. She always told me that she wanted to be fair to my father, but whenever anything upset me, she would always think it was him.

"No, Mom, it's not Dad," I said.

"Was it that thing he said about a tie not being good enough?" she asked. "You know he's so competitive, sometimes he doesn't realize what he's saying."

"Mom, he was right about that. A tie isn't good enough. Even Uncle Beef said a tie stinks."

"Winning isn't everything," said Mom.

I rolled my eyes.

"Don't give me that look," she snapped.

"Sorry," I muttered. "It's just that you've never played football."

"And that makes you think I don't understand you," said Mom, her voice rising. "I know how much you love to win. Honey, you didn't just get that from your father. I hate to lose too." Loving to win was very different from hating to lose. I had both in me.

When we got home, I went into the bathroom to take a hot shower. As the water poured over me I began to relive the moment that I had run down the field and charged into Miranda. I wish I could say that I felt bad about it, but I didn't. I kept thinking about Uncle Beef saying to me, *Why don't you play on my team . . . ?* All right, I knew it wasn't the same thing as running onto the turf at Rich Stadium. Still, I would be able to put on pads and a helmet, something I had never gotten to do in Peewee.

I got out of the shower and toweled off. I pulled on a pair of shorts and a T-shirt, and turned on my computer.

It had barely warmed up when I got an Instant Message from Molly.

"I THINK WE SHOULD TRY OUT!" she typed. I couldn't

tell if Molly was really that excited or if she had just hit the Caps Lock by mistake.

"Do you really think so?" I asked her.

"I talked to my folks about it," she wrote. "They said middle school is the only time to try."

"Your folks don't sound like mine," I replied. "Mine don't want me to play. In fact, Dad's worse about it than Mom."

"Your dad?" asked Molly, surprised. "I'd think that he'd love to see you play. And besides, your dad's great. He'll do anything that he thinks is good for you."

"Molly . . ." I started to write. Then I realized that I couldn't explain Dad to her, especially in an Instant Message.

"You're right," I typed, wishing that we could talk in person. Then I signed off.

It was as if Molly was psychic. The phone rang. "You don't sound as excited as you should be," she said.

"You could tell that just from my message?" I asked.

"Yes," she said. "Your typing sounds depressed. How come you're not so psyched?"

"Well, my dad seems to think it's a really bad idea," I said. "So does my mom."

"That doesn't usually stop you," said Molly.

I giggled. Somehow talking to Molly made everything so much less serious.

"You're right," I said. "I'll try out if you will."

"You've got it," said Molly.

I thought about what Eric had said about working out with weights. "Want to go to the Y and work out this weekend before the tryouts?" I asked her.

"Sure," said Molly. "But do you think we need the work-out, or do you just want to hang out with Eric?"

"Molly!" I exclaimed.

"Come on . . . slim hips, wide shoulders? Just remember—he's a running back and so are you."

"What are you saying?" I asked Molly.

"Maybe you two will collide . . . and I don't just mean on the football field."

"I don't like Eric that way," I said.

"You sure?" Molly asked.

"Do you think he likes me that way?" I asked.

"Maybe," said Molly. "He sure shook his pom-poms in your direction."

"That was Oscar," I said, giggling.

"Yeah, well, you didn't notice, but Eric was shaking them too."

"Really?"

"Really," said Molly.

I wasn't exactly sure why. But that night I went to bed smiling.

IT'S JUST A BLACK EYE

WHEN DAD PICKED ME UP ON SATURDAY I TOLD him I wanted to go to the Y to work out that afternoon. "Molly and I are going together. We're psyched for the tryouts on Monday."

Dad stared at me. "You didn't really take Beef seriously, did you?"

"That's nice, Dad," I said. "He's supposed to be your best friend. Are you suggesting he was putting Molly and me on when he asked us to try out?"

"I'm sorry. It's just that it seems ridiculous to me."

"Going to the Y or trying out?"

"Trying out. I'm happy to take you to the Y."

"That's so supportive."

"I'm sorry," Dad said quickly. "But actually, are you sure you want to go to the Y today? You shouldn't do a heavy workout if you want to be at the top of your game for the tryouts."

I looked at him. Was he actually saying that because he wanted me to make the team?

"So you're not against my trying out?" I asked.

"I don't want us to get into a fight about this," said Dad. "Let's not let it ruin our weekend. I'll take you to the Y after lunch."

It was a noncommittal answer, but I decided to take it.

When we walked into the house, Jason was just getting up from his morning nap. He came at me carrying his soft football.

I grinned at him. "You want to play a little tackle football?" I asked.

He giggled.

"Do you want me to take him outside to play?" I asked Serena. "It's a pretty day."

"That would be great," said Serena. Jason held on to his Nerf ball, and I picked up my regulation Buffalo Bills football. We went out to the grass in front of their townhouse.

Jason tried to throw the ball at me. He fell down and laughed. Then he jumped up, put the ball up near his ear, and gave it his all. The ball squiggled out of his hand and dropped to the ground.

"Fumble!" I shouted. It's one of Jason's favorite words.

I fell on the ball. Jason jumped on me, tackling me.

I tickled him.

"No fair tickling the quarterback," joked Dad. I hadn't seen him come outside.

"Okay, everybody pile on Dad," I shouted to Jason. We both tried to bring down Dad. But he stiffened his legs. He wasn't going to fall down without a fight. I pushed harder, grabbing at his knees. Jason stood to the side, as if realizing that suddenly this wasn't just a silly game.

I pushed with all my strength. Dad pushed back. Then somehow I got my arms wrapped around him at the right angle, and he fell. Jason and I jumped on top of him.

"Whoa!" said Dad. "Time out! You gave me a snot bubble!" I looked up. Snot was coming out of Dad's nose. I hadn't realized I had landed on him that hard.

"Are you okay?" I asked.

Dad laughed. "It's not the first snot bubble I've gotten. It's just the first from my daughter."

"What's a snot bubble?" I asked him.

"It's when the linebacker hits you so hard with his helmet that the snot literally bubbles out of your nose," Dad explained. He stood up, brushed himself off, and wiped his nose.

"I'm not afraid of a little snot bubble," I said, making it into a song. Jason laughed, but Dad didn't.

"What if somebody like Oscar lands on you?" asked Dad.

"He's on my team, remember?" I said.

"You'll be playing against people his size. And not with a little soft football, either."

Serena came out on the porch. Jason ran up to her. She picked him up. "My, you're a smelly little thing," she said. "I'd better change you." I felt a little guilty, as if I should have noticed that his diaper was poopy. Usually I'm good about that.

Dad watched Serena go inside with Jason. "Football is a rough game," said Dad. "You have to stay focused every minute. And if you lose that focus, you can get hurt." He picked up the regulation ball, backed up, and threw it at me.

I caught it. "That's very nice, Dad. Are you saying that girls aren't focused? Or just me?" I flung the ball back to him.

"I love you. I just don't want to see you hurt," he said.

I sighed. "Wouldn't you let Jason play when he grows up?" I asked him, as he tossed the ball to me.

"We'll cross that bridge when we come to it."

"You used to say that humans love trying something difficult," I said to him. I threw the ball back so hard I could tell it stung his hands.

"There's such a thing as trying something that's too difficult," said Dad, throwing a tight spiral right at my knees. I caught it.

"Maybe for you," I said. "But that doesn't mean it's true for me." We both stopped talking.

We tossed the ball back and forth. It was as if the football were on a taut string between us. We stopped talking. I liked it that way. When Dad and I did something physical together, we were fine. I knew it made Mom uncomfortable that Dad didn't talk more. She said she never knew what he was thinking. But Mom doesn't know the pleasure of focusing on something like a ball heading for your hands. Your mind does go blank.

Then *boink!* As soon as I started thinking about how much I liked the silence, I ruined it. Dad threw the ball to me and, instead of catching it, my hands flew apart, and the end of the ball hit me in the eye, hard.

My hand flew up to my eye automatically. For a second, I couldn't see.

"Are you okay?" Dad shouted.

I waved him off. My eye was tearing.

Dad ran to me. "Let me see your eye." He could barely pry my hand away from my face.

"I'm fine."

Dad gently pulled my hand away from my eye and looked at it. "You probably are," he said. "Let's go inside and put ice on it."

We went into the house. "Oh my, what happened?" asked Serena.

"Cassie tried to catch the football with her eye," said Dad.

"I'm fine!" I repeated. I could barely see Serena. She ran to the freezer and took out the container of ice.

Dad got a Ziploc bag and put some ice in it. He gave me the bag covered with a cloth napkin to hold up to my eye.

Jason stood by my knee, looking worried. "I'm fine," I whispered to him. I loved it that he cared.

"No wonder your father doesn't want you to play football," said Serena. I glared at her through my good eye.

"Let me see it," said Dad. I lifted the ice pack from my face.

"Your eye looks fine. It just hit the fleshy part around your socket. It's already turning colors, but you'll be fine."

"It doesn't hurt that much," I lied.

"A black eye is nothing," said Dad. "Football players have to play with a lot of pain. Once I broke my collarbone during a game, and I played the whole quarter."

My eye was still swelling.

I stood up. "Are you feeling better?" he asked softly.

"Sure, Dad," I said. "It's just a black eye."

Dad kissed me gently on my eyelid. I'm tall enough that he can do that when we're both standing up straight. His kiss actually did make it feel better.

I THINK I KNOW BETTER THAN YOU

WHEN WE GOT TO THE Y, DAD WAS ALL SMILES. HE was in his element. Dad had probably spent half his life in the weight room at the Y. Almost everybody there knew him.

"Hey, Geoff," said one of the trainers, a well-built man with a shaved head.

"Hi, Dave," said Dad. "You know my daughter, don't you?"

"Sure," said Dave, "she's here all the time with her mom." I grinned. Maybe Dave would ask Mom out sometime.

Dad told me he was going to warm up and asked if I wanted to run around the track with him. I was about to say yes, when I saw Molly standing and laughing with Oscar and Eric.

"You go, Dad," I said. "There's Molly."

Dad started to do some stretches, and I saw a few women turn to watch him as the powerful muscles in his legs contracted and released.

He smiled at them, his blue eyes twinkling. Dad was a natural flirt. He did it as easily as breathing. Mom used to talk about the way girls flocked around him. I walked away.

Molly stared at my black eye. "Where did you get that?" she asked.

"Is that from the Powderpuff game?" Oscar asked.

"No, I just got it this morning. I was playing with Jason, and then Dad and I were tossing the football around, and I caught the football with my face."

"Yeah, I've done that," said Oscar.

"Yeah, but on you a black eye is kind of normal," said Eric. "Cassie looks like she's wearing the wrong kind of makeup."

"Oh," Molly teased. "You mean the kind you were wearing on Thursday was the *right* kind?"

"So, is the rumor true?" asked Eric. "Did Coach Harris really ask you girls to try out?"

"He did," said Molly. "And we're doing it. I'm going out for kicker and Cassie's trying for running back. Your position."

"Well, we do need a kicker," admitted Eric. "But, Cassie, you'd be flattened if you played with us."

"I don't think so, Eric," I said.

Eric sat down on the lat machine. The weight was set at one hundred pounds. He grunted as he pulled the bar down. He did eight reps. The machine banged as he stopped.

"You want to try?" he asked.

"Yeah," I said. I put the pin at sixty, a weight I knew I could handle.

I leaned back and put my stomach muscles into pulling down the bar.

"Good form," said Oscar.

"Lightweight," said Eric.

"I like to warm up my muscles," I explained.

We did a circuit of the machines in the room, and I kept to weights I could handle. Then we came to the bench press.

"You warmed up now?" taunted Eric. "Do you want to lift some real weights?"

He slipped two twenty-pound weights on either end of the bar.

"Don't do it, Cassie. You could hurt yourself," warned Oscar.

I got in position under the bar. I put my hands on it. I tried to set myself, but I knew that it was heavier than I could press.

Oscar looked down at me. "When the weight is heavy, just breathe deeper."

I nodded. Then, taking his advice, I took a deep breath and pushed the bar away from me. The weight was heavy, but I could get it over my chest. Oscar hovered above me, carefully spotting me.

On my fourth rep, my arms began to shake. Oscar took the weight.

"I need it a little lighter," I admitted.

I'm not a wimp, but I knew that if I tried to lift a weight that was too heavy, I could really hurt myself, and then it would be good-bye to the tryouts.

"I'll lift it soon," I said.

"Oh, sure," said Eric.

"She's being smart," said Oscar, as he settled himself on the bench.

I watched him. As he strained to lift the weight, Oscar's face was concentrated, but oddly handsome. And I usually didn't think of Oscar as handsome.

"Good one, Oscar," said Molly as he finished eight reps.

Oscar smiled at her shyly. I had always thought that Oscar liked Ella, but the way he was looking at Molly made me wonder.

Eric glanced over at me. "Can you do real push-ups, Cassie?" he asked. "Coach Harris loves to make us do push-ups. You quit Peewee before we began playing tackle football. He got much tougher. If you drop a handoff, it's ten push-ups. If you try to tackle with your head down, twenty. Let me see your push-ups."

I got into the push-up position. I may not be able to lift heavy weights, but upper-body strength is really important for sprints. I did six quick push-ups with my knees off the ground.

Oscar helped me up. "Pretty unbelievable," said Oscar.

I stared at him. "My doing push-ups or trying out for the team?"

"Both," said Oscar. "It *is* pretty unbelievable that you're really trying out for the team." Something in his voice made me doubt he meant "unbelievable" in a good way.

"Don't you think it's a good idea?" I pushed. "After all, when we play in your backyard, you tell me I'm terrific all the time."

"Games with other schools are different. Most of the teams don't have girls on them."

I bit my lip. In my fantasy, Oscar would say, *Go for it, girl!* But he didn't.

"I'm strong," I reminded him.

"I know," said Oscar. "But you're still a girl."

"Let's do the leg presses," I said. I knew my legs were strong. I put the weight at one hundred pounds. I had done that weight before. Just then Dad came up to us. He looked at the weight and said, "Stop. You'll hurt yourself."

"I'm fine," I told him.

"That's much too heavy for you," said Dad.

"No, it isn't," I argued. My dad was making me nervous. I tried to push the weight with my quads, but I didn't exhale at the right moment, and without the power from my diaphragm, the weight wouldn't budge.

"Listen to me," argued Dad. "I think I know better than you what you can and can't do."

Oscar looked embarrassed for me. "Cassie, maybe you shouldn't try to do too much."

"Don't tell me what you think I *can't* do," I snapped.

Oscar put up both his hands as if to guard himself against me.

"Whoa . . . ," he said. "I'm the one who's been arguing with Eric and the other guys that you might be good on the team. It's just a lot to digest, you know?"

"See," said Dad. "If even Oscar is having trouble with it, you know it's not a good idea."

I pushed the weight up with my legs and got it to move, but not smoothly. I didn't know why, but suddenly a weight that I could usually lift felt too heavy.

TRYOUTS

MY EYE WAS STILL MULTICOLORED ON MONDAY. Apparently the rumor mill was going full tilt. "Hey," said Ella when she saw me at my locker. "I heard you got that black eye trying to play football with the boys."

"That's not how it happened," I said, fiddling with my lock. "Where did you hear that?"

"It's all over school," Ella said.

I rolled my good eye. "I don't believe it. I hate this," I said. "Molly and I haven't even tried out, and people are already spreading rumors that the boys gave me a black eye just for thinking about it. I got this playing football with my dad."

Ella laughed. "So the rumors aren't completely wrong," she teased.

"What are you talking about?" I asked her.

"Well, you can't be a girl playing football and not expect people to talk," she said.

I stared at her. "You were the one who encouraged Molly and me to do this."

"Yeah, and I still think it's a good idea," said Ella. "But

you'd better be prepared to take some flak." We went into our homeroom together.

The day seemed to drag on. Everyone asked me about my black eye. Finally Molly and I went to the gym to sign up for the tryouts. We thought there would be a huge crowd. But there wasn't. There were very few new eighth graders trying out, and among the seventh graders, there were just about twenty-five of us. Twenty-three boys and two girls.

"Cassie?" asked Coach Harris. "How did you get that black eye?"

"From a football," I said. "I tried to catch one of my dad's passes with my eye."

"Oh," he said. "Well, out here we try to catch the football with our hands." The group laughed.

"Listen up," said Coach Harris. "All of you know that Molly and Cassie are trying out. I know the school's been talking about it all day. We've even talked about it in the teachers' lounge. The administration is behind my decision and respects it. I want you to show Molly and Cassie respect too."

"Why should they get more respect than anybody else?" asked Brant. There was a challenge in his tone.

"Not more—just the same," Coach Harris firmly said. "All right, everybody. Let's loosen up. Jog once around the field."

We took off. Unlike at a track team workout, the boys seemed to be going very slowly. I wasn't used to such an unhurried pace, and I soon found myself out in front with Eric.

"I can't believe you and Molly really showed up," he said.

"We told you we were going to do it at the Y. What would make you think we changed our minds?"

Eric shook his head. "Look, this isn't touch football. We play tackle. And you've never played tackle."

"Look, I quit Peewee because my dad got married and stopped being interested. It was a stupid reason to quit, and now I'm getting a second chance. I always loved it."

"It's going to get rough," warned Eric.

"I can take it," I said. "I've had plenty of snot bubbles."

Eric looked down at me, as if he could tell I was making it up. "How do you know what a snot bubble is?" he asked.

I didn't answer him. I didn't want him to know that I had just learned the term over the weekend. I put on a burst of speed and passed him as we rounded the corner.

"Slow it down," shouted Coach Harris. "This isn't a race. It's a warm-up."

Coach Harris blew his whistle and gathered us in a circle around him. "Let's do some stretches." He had us stand on one foot and stretch our hamstrings by pulling the other foot up to our butt. In yoga, it's called the standing bird. The guys looked like awkward storks, tottering a little, and Molly and I could hold the stretch longer than most of them.

After our stretches, we did wind sprints. As we went through the drills, I was dripping sweat. So far, I knew that I was at least as good as most of the other boys—even Eric.

Next, Coach Harris sent two of us out at a time, flying down the field as fast as we could. He heaved the ball, and both people had to try to get it. It was a lot like the game Oscar and I played in his backyard, except this time it wasn't just for fun. It was to make the team.

Eric and I were the last pair to be sent out. Then Coach Harris shouted, "Go get it!" We both jumped up at the same second. Eric's taller than I am, but I was just a split second faster, and I got my hands on the ball first. I gathered it in. Eric tried to bat it away from me. We fell over fighting for it.

I thought once we were on the ground he had to quit trying to take it away. But Eric kept clawing at me and eventually got the ball out of my hands. He stood up with it.

"I had it first!" I complained. I looked around for Coach Harris but he was over on the sidelines looking for something in the huge shed where they keep the equipment.

"It's the one who's got it last who wins!" said Eric. "Welcome to real football," he added. "It's a good day for the faint of heart to go home." He headed for the sidelines.

"I'm not going home," I muttered. I picked myself up and followed him.

Coach Harris kicked about half a dozen big balance balls out of the shed.

"This looks like fun," I said.

"Wait," said Oscar. "It's harder than it looks."

I watched the guys who went first. I saw what he meant. Coach Harris placed the ball between two players. They had to push against each other, keeping the ball between them while running forward or backward.

I was paired with Harold, an African-American boy I didn't know very well. The ball was already sweaty from the others who had gone before us. I knew Harold played defense.

"You ever done this before?" Harold asked.

I shook my head no. I wiped the hair out of my eyes.

The whistle blew. Harold and I found a rhythm running with both our hands on the ball.

Then Coach Harris yelled, "Resist!"

Suddenly I felt Harold put his weight behind the ball, but I leaned back and kept my feet moving quickly in choppy steps. The ball began to slip to the side, but we both kept our hands on it. I was gaining a little, pushing Harold backward.

"Look what we have here!" shouted Coach Harris. "It's a standoff!" Harold was straining. I pushed against the ball.

"Okay!" Coach Harris shouted. "Reverse!" This meant that now Harold got to push forward and I had to run backward, holding the ball between us. Harold was running quickly so I had to keep my feet moving in short little steps, and I had to be careful not to fall over backward.

We got about halfway across the field when I heard the shout "Resist!" Harold instantly began pushing hard against me. I tried to plant my feet to stop him, but as soon as I did, I fell.

I landed hard on my butt, and my head hit the grass.

"Are you okay?" Harold asked. Sweat was running down his face and landing on me.

"Yeah," I said, although I felt woozy. Harold leaned down and gave me his right hand.

I took it and started to sit up. Suddenly I felt nauseated and threw up all over Harold's shoes.

"Oh, yuck!" shouted Harold, jumping out of the way.

Coach Harris ran over to us. He thrust his hand toward my face, with his thumb folded down. "How many fingers do I have up?" he said.

"Four," I said.

"What's your name?"

"Cassie," I said. "And you're Uncle Beef, Coach Harris."

"Is she all right?" Harold asked.

Coach Harris nodded. "Harold, why don't you go wash off your shoes? I'll take care of Cassie."

"I'm fine," I said.

Coach Harris helped me to the bench and gave me some ice to suck. "I want you to sit here quietly. Do you know what you did wrong?"

"Yeah, I fell," I said.

"Do you know why you fell?"

I shook my head no. It hurt a little. "Sorry," I muttered.

"Don't be sorry, but you fell because you stopped moving your feet. When you were pushing against Harold up the field, you kept your feet going, and that's why you gained momentum. As soon as he began to push against you, you stopped moving your feet. You stop moving, and you're dead. . . ."

"Like a shark," I said.

"That's right," said Harold, who had come back and was standing over me. His shoes were wet. "That's how sharks keep alive. Sharks can travel really fast, faster than most meat-eating fish. Most fish have a swim bladder that's full of gas. Sharks don't have a swim bladder. They've got a large liver—and it's filled with oil. See, oil is lighter than water, and it helps the shark keep from sinking, but even so, most sharks have to swim all the time or they will sink."

Coach Harris laughed. "Harold, if you have that much energy to talk to Cassie about sharks, you've got enough energy to go back out there with the others and give me twenty push-ups and then forty sit-ups. Let's see if you can keep from sinking after that. Cassie, you stay on the bench."

Coach Harris didn't let me get up for the rest of the try-outs. I was really worried. I had barely been able to show him what I could do. I watched Molly do the ball exercise against a seventh grader who didn't even weigh as much as she did. She wiped the field with him.

As we walked back toward the locker rooms, I got in line with Harold. "I'm sorry about your shoes," I said.

"That stuff happens," he said.

"I liked what you said about the sharks."

Harold shrugged.

"What do you think about Molly and me trying out for the football team?"

"The other teams don't have girls on them." Both he and Oscar had made the exact same point. I hadn't realized that it would bother them quite so much.

"It's not as if I've never played," I argued. "Coach Harris once told me that I had an innate instinct for finding my way upfield."

Harold shrugged. "How long ago was that?" he asked.

"Well, I was only seven or eight. But if I showed that kind of talent, then it must mean something."

"Maybe," said Harold. He didn't sound convinced. Harold

reminded me of my dad. He wasn't being mean. He was just stating facts the way he saw them, but he wasn't saying what I wanted him to say.

I wanted him to say, *Even though you threw up on my shoes, I admire your guts.* Harold seemed like a good guy, and even *he* didn't want me on the team. After watching me throw up, I wondered if Uncle Beef agreed with him.

KNOW WHAT YOU'RE GETTING INTO!

STANDING INSIDE THE GIRLS' LOCKER ROOM, I felt the back of my head. There was a lump under my hair that felt tender to the touch. I had to be careful as I shampooed because my scalp hurt.

As I stepped out of the shower, Molly was naked in front of me. She was grinning. "Well, was that a hoot or what?" she said. "Did you see me kick the ball? I made three out of five. Poor Oscar had to hold the ball for me, and I could tell he was scared I was going to kick his fingers, or maybe even kick his head, but I was great!"

She stepped under the hot spray. Molly's breasts are much smaller than mine; maybe that's why she was so unselfconscious naked. I was only in fifth grade when I started having to wear a bra all the time. Now I wear a C cup.

"Didn't you love it?" continued Molly.

"Love what?"

"Being the only two girls out there. It was fun." She stepped out of the shower. I handed her a towel. "You're being awfully quiet," she said.

"I guess I didn't expect you to come out so gung-ho," I said.

"It was just more fun than I expected," she answered.

I rubbed the towel over my head, drying my hair. I flinched.

"What's wrong?" she asked. "Why did you make that face?"

"I fell and hit my head doing that ball thing with Harold. I didn't keep moving. Harold gave me a lecture on the bladder of a shark."

"He likes facts," said Molly. "He's like a walking encyclopedia on all animals. He's in my French class."

"Great! Maybe he can teach me the word for vomit in French since I threw up on his shoes."

"*Vomissure*," said Molly. "It's a feminine noun. Did you know *brassiere* is a masculine word? You should have heard the guys giggle. But French is all topsy-turvy. That's why I like it."

We walked arm in arm out of the girls' locker room. Ella was waiting for us in the hallway. She put her hands up and gave Molly a high five.

"I made the cheerleading team. How were your try-outs?" Ella asked. "A triumph?"

Molly grinned. "I kicked more balls through the goal-posts than anybody else. And Cassie's always been good."

"I can't wait till you get the uniforms," said Ella. "Football uniforms are even cuter than cheerleading costumes—those tight pants. I always wondered what goes on in those huddles. You'll be able to give the rest of us girls the inside scoop."

"Cassie and I could write a column for the newspaper called 'Girls' Inside Track'! Get it? It's a pun because we both run track in the spring," Molly said.

I hoped she was kidding. "We can't tell what goes on in the huddle. It's sacred. The way you win a football game is keeping secrets from the other teams and having sneak plays. We can't ruin the strategy. The guys would never trust us."

"I was kidding," said Molly.

"What's up with Cassie?" Ella asked Molly.

"She fell on her head," Molly explained. "I think she fell on her sense-of-humor button. It's turned off."

I grimaced. "Sorry," I muttered. "I didn't realize you were kidding."

"Actually, I wasn't completely," said Ella. "I'm kind of hoping that you two will give us the inside scoop on the boys."

"*If* we make the team," I said. "So far my only inside scoops are that Harold knows a lot about sharks and most of the guys don't think we should be playing."

"It's not what *they* think that counts. It's what Coach Harris thinks," Ella reminded me. "I don't think he would have asked you to try out if he didn't think you had a decent chance."

"We'll find out tomorrow," said Molly. "Coach Harris doesn't waste any time. He has the tryouts, and then he posts the roster the next morning. There are a bunch of eighth-grade varsity players who we know will make the team, but there should be room for at least fifteen new kids. At least we don't have to wait long. Coach Harris doesn't believe in kids worrying all day whether they've made the team. I bet Cassie and I will make it."

Molly sounded so confident, but I didn't feel as sure. How weird would it be if Molly made the team, and I didn't?

When I got home, I asked Mom for a couple of Advil. She looked worried. "What's wrong?"

"Nothing," I said. "I just feel a little achy. At the tryouts, I used muscles I haven't used in a while. It's no biggie. . . ."

Before I could finish the sentence the phone rang.

Mom picked it up. "Hi, Beef," she said. Mom has a certain warmth in her voice when she talks to Uncle Beef. But then her tone turned serious.

"What? She didn't tell me anything about it." Mom turned to me. "Uncle Beef wants to know how your head is. He said you fell pretty hard today."

"Tell him I'm fine," I said.

"He wants to talk to you," she said. She handed the phone to me.

"Just checking up on you," said Uncle Beef. "Any double vision or headache? Any nausea?"

"None," I said truthfully. "My head just has a lump on it."

"Do you have an appetite?" he asked.

"Yeah, I'm hungry," I admitted, surprised at how hungry I was.

"Good, because we're having a barbecue this weekend. Put your mom back on. I want to invite her officially."

I gave the phone back to Mom. She listened. "No, that's

fine with me. I'd love to come. I'll make my potato salad."

Mom makes one of the best potato salads in the world. It's a recipe she got from her mother.

She hung up. "When were you going to tell me about clunking your head?" she asked. "Is that why you needed Advil?"

"It really wasn't a big deal," I said.

"Look," she said. "If you're going to be playing football, I need you to be honest with me. I remember when your dad played. It was a macho thing to never admit he was injured. And it hurt him. He ended up needing both shoulder and knee surgeries in college. He kept postponing them, and it hurts him every day as a result."

"I didn't know that," I said. "Dad never talks about it."

"You've seen the way he limps when he first gets out of bed in the morning. That's why he needs to stand in the shower for fifteen minutes."

"I just thought he was very clean," I said. "And later I thought it was because he had been drinking. After he told us that he had a drinking problem."

Mom shook her head. "No. It was old football injuries. I sometimes wondered if that's why he started drinking, because he was in pain all the time in high school and college. I don't want that for you."

"Mom, I'm not going to drink. I haven't even made the team, and you're already having me limping for the rest of my life."

"I just want to be sure you know what you're getting into," said Mom.

In the morning, I felt better. My muscles ached, but not my head, as long as I didn't touch the lump, and even that felt much smaller.

Of course, Mom was still worried. She poked her head into my room. "How are you?"

"I'm fine," I said. I rolled out of bed.

"No headaches?" She sounded worried.

I shook my head. Mom watched me carefully for a grimace, but it really didn't hurt.

"Honest, I'm fine," I said. "Really." And I meant it.

"Good," said Mom.

I got dressed and joined Mom for breakfast.

"I find out if I made the team this morning," I told her.

"I still can't believe you're thinking of playing that game."

"You never called it 'that game' before," I said. "You sound a little like Serena. You know, she hates football."

Mom looked at me. I don't usually mention Serena around her, certainly not to make comparisons.

"This doesn't have to do with football as a game," said Mom. "It has to do with my daughter playing a game that girls don't usually play."

"Did it bother you when I played Peewee football?" I asked her. "You used to come to all the games."

"No," said Mom. "But that was a different time. When you were younger, you were so excited to be doing something that your dad did. I just figured you would naturally outgrow it."

"My playing football now isn't about Dad, Mom. He doesn't want me to play any more than you do."

Mom nodded. "Well, let's not argue about it," she said. That was her way of saying she didn't agree with me, and she never would. She gave me a kiss. I got my backpack and walked out the door.

When the bus picked me up, Molly had once again saved a seat for me.

"Hey, Cassie," shouted Harold from the back of the bus. "How's your head?"

"Fine," I told him.

"You ready to find out whether you made the team?" asked Harold. "It'll be on the bulletin board outside of the gym."

"I know," I said. "Harold, I've known Coach Harris longer than you have."

Harold looked away.

"You didn't have to snap his head off," Molly said. "Are you nervous? You never had to worry about making a team before. I'm not worried."

I couldn't believe that Molly wasn't nervous and I was. Usually I was such a good athlete that I knew I would make whatever team I tried out for. I could basically be on any girls' team I wanted. But this was different.

Ella was waiting for us at the school's main entrance.

"I thought we should go together to see," she said. "I want to be there for this historic moment."

"What's historic about it?" I asked.

"My two best girl friends playing football."

"Or one of your girl friends not making the team," I muttered.

Ella looked at Molly. "What's up with her?" she asked.

"She's got a case of nerves," said Molly.

Ella wrapped her arm around my elbow. "Come on, Cassie—I want to see you do what you always talked about doing."

Everybody in school seemed to stare as we walked down to the gym. I could see a group gathered in front of the bulletin board including Harold, Oscar, Eric, and Brant. Tommy Zaworski gave me a dirty look as he walked away.

Oscar turned. "Well, you two made history," he said. He didn't sound as if he thought it was a good thing.

Molly pushed her way up front to read it for herself, and then she hugged me.

"Hey, guys!" shouted Molly to Harold, Brant, Oscar, and Eric. "We're your teammates."

"Oh, we're so excited," said Eric sarcastically.

"You *are* part of history," said Molly, poking him in the ribs. "You'll be the first boys to play football with girls in Clarence."

"Yeah, that's really the way we want to be remembered," said Eric.

"You didn't have a winning season last year," I argued. "So maybe with us on the team you will. That'll surprise people more than having girls on the team."

"I may break the record for field goals," said Molly. "I've got to find out what it is."

Harold just shook his head. "Wait till you get in a real

game before you talk about breaking records," he warned her.

"Hey, Molly," said Eric. "I've got a football joke for you. Did you hear about the kicker who was so bad, he missed a field goal? Then he got mad and went to kick himself in the pants, and he missed that too! Maybe you'll be that bad."

"Yeah, Eric," said Molly. "I notice your number is 53. I guess they gave that to you so you wouldn't forget your IQ."

Eric laughed. "So, will you and Cassie try to get the number 0? To match the number of other girls you'll see on the field—and the number of points you'll rack up?"

"That's not funny!" I said angrily.

"Cool it," whispered Molly. "He's just teasing."

"Cut it out, everybody," said Oscar. "Dad wouldn't have put Cassie and Molly on the team if they weren't good enough."

"Thanks, Oscar," I said.

"You'd better be nice to him," warned Harold. "He's going to be the only thing standing between you and disaster."

Molly passed me some pieces of paper. "Here are the consent forms. They need to be signed before our first game. I got a couple for you."

"What about your parents?" I asked her. "Are you sure that they'll sign without a problem?"

"Yes," said Molly. "What are you worried about? Both your parents are friends with Coach Harris. They trust him."

"Right," I muttered. "It'll be a piece of cake. Playing boys' football."

"Stop calling it boys' football," insisted Molly. "It's football! After school today we'll be fitted for our uniforms. Once we have our helmets on, nobody will know whether we're girls or boys."

"We'll know," I reminded her. "And I think everybody else is going to know too."

REAL FOOTBALL PLAYERS WEAR GIRDLES

THAT AFTERNOON, MOLLY AND I WENT DOWN TO the gym to get our uniforms. "Girdles here! Pants over there!" yelled the assistant coach. "The pads are on that table to the left! Get your shoulder pads fitted and then your helmet and your brain pad. Be sure to take your brain pad home and boil it and fit it! Let's move, people!"

"Girdles, brain pad," whispered Molly. "What *are* these things?" I was as lost as Molly. It was extremely embarrassing to have to admit that after bragging about playing football all my life, I had no idea. I had never worn football equipment. When I played Peewee football we never put on pads or a helmet—or any of this gear. I couldn't believe how much of it there was.

"I don't know," I admitted. "Girdles? I thought those were something my grandmother wore."

"Molly, Cassie, stop holding up the line," shouted Coach Harris. "I don't want to spend all day on this. Get your stuff, go to the girls' locker room, and then come meet us out on the field."

Soon our arms were piled high with gear. Besides all the pads, we each had nylon pants that looked like bike shorts, and another pair of polyester pants that looked like capri pants with a lot of panels on them.

"Who knew football players wore two pairs of pants?" Molly giggled.

"Putting on the pants looks easy," I said. "But look at this." I held up the shoulder pads. They had so many buckles and ties that they looked like something you'd wear in a gladiator movie.

I tried to carry it all in my arms, but it was piled past my nose and I could barely see. I saw the guys stick their helmets through the hole for their heads in their shoulder pads.

They looked cool, but when I tried to do the same thing with my helmet, it got stuck. Eric laughed at me. Then Oscar came over and jammed the helmet through the pads. He handed the whole contraption to me, then did the same with Molly's gear.

Molly and I went into the girls' locker room to try to make sense of it all. We piled the entire collection on a bench. "So what do we do with all this?" Molly asked.

I didn't have the slightest idea. Molly picked up the pants that everybody called a girdle. They looked like long bike shorts.

"Eureka!" she shouted. "They've got slots in them. They must be where the pads go. Who knew football players wore girdles?"

I giggled. We spent about fifteen minutes trying to jam

the different-size pads into the holes sewn into the inside of the pants. The pads kept popping out.

There was a knock on the locker room door. Harold shouted, "Coach Harris says you two are taking too long."

"Well, this stuff should come with directions," I wailed.

"I thought you knew all about this," said Molly. She looked disappointed in me.

I took a deep breath. "Both my parents say you only look stupid if you're stupid enough not to ask questions," I said. I hitched up the girdle thing with the pads sticking out of my hips. "Let's go."

"Where?" asked Molly.

"Out onto the field. We've got to ask how to get into all of this."

"You don't even have the pants on," Molly argued.

I looked down at myself. "Molly, this girdle thing covers up three times as much as our track uniforms. Come on!"

Molly pulled at her waistband and grabbed her stuff, and we ran out onto the field.

Eric was laughing at us. "Hey, girls, a full-uniform practice means we *wear* our pants; we don't carry them."

"Ignore him," I warned Molly.

I went up to Coach Harris. "Excuse me, Coach," I said. "We're having trouble."

Coach Harris didn't laugh at us. "You've never worn a full uniform before. Okay, the hip pads go here. They protect your kidneys." He adjusted the biggest pads by my hips. The pads came up to beyond my waist and they were held tightly in place by the latex of the girdle.

"Now, the thigh pads and the knee pads go in the pockets of the outer pants," he explained.

There were still two pads left over, both of them long and thin. One was hard and the other was made out of the same foam material as the other pads.

Coach Harris laughed. "I don't think you need the cup," he said, "but the tail pad is one of the most important ones. Never play without it, and always be sure it goes in right."

I giggled nervously. "Cut it out. I used to diaper you as a baby," said Coach Harris. He showed me how to jam the tail pad in a pocket of the girdle so it fit snugly from my waist to the tip of my tailbone.

"Now, put on your pants over the girdle. Go over to Ben, our new equipment manager, and get your shoulder pads and helmet adjusted."

I was already sweating just from the tightness of the pants and the unfamiliar feel of the pads.

"Molly," said Coach Harris, "I'll fix yours today, but from now on, girls, you put on your own pants."

After Molly got fitted, we ran over to get our shoulder pads fixed. It was easy for Molly because she's fairly flat-chested, but for me it took a lot of adjustment to get the big shoulder pads to fit right.

"I don't think any other equipment guy has this problem," said Ben, an eighth grader I had never met before. I ignored the fact that he was blushing as he tried to hook the straps from the back under my arms and into the front of the big shoulder pads. Finally we were ready for our helmets.

"Here's your brain pad. It's like a mouth guard, only

better," said Ben, handing me something that looked like a dental retainer. "It does more than just protect your teeth. It keeps your head from getting jarred. You've got to wear it for every play." It was in a plastic container, and it already had my name on it. "It hooks on to your helmet, so you can spit it out in between plays or if you're on the bench." Ben showed me how to hook it to my face mask.

"Got it," I said. I tried to put on the helmet. I couldn't pry it open to get it over my ears.

Ben sighed and showed me how to put my fingers through the ear holes to pry it loose. Finally I was dressed.

Coach Harris blew his whistle. "Okay, just take an easy jog around the field." With all the equipment on, I could barely move. Halfway around the field, I felt sweat running down my waist and soaking into the pads, all of which were digging into me.

When we finished, we did our stretches and calisthenics. Then we separated into the offensive and defensive teams. Molly went with the special teams, the kickers and the players who run the ball after kickoffs. I felt much more alone without her.

"Line up!" shouted Coach Harris to our offensive team. "Let's do some handoff drills." Brant tried to hand the ball to me, but I didn't grab it tightly and the ball went bouncing out.

"Ten push-ups, Cassie," yelled Coach Harris.

"Does she get to do the girlie ones?" Eric asked.

"No," shouted Coach Harris. "Drop, Cassie."

I dropped to the grass and assumed the push-up position.

My head felt incredibly awkward with the helmet on. But I did ten without my knees touching the ground once. I stood up. At least my shoulder pads hid the fact that my biceps were trembling.

Coach Harris just grunted, and we went on with the practice. We began running simple plays. I was fine for the first three. On the third play, I was supposed to be the decoy for Eric. Harold thought I had the ball and went to tackle me, but I dove for his legs and got to him before he could get to me. We both tumbled to the ground hard.

"Good one, Cassie," shouted Coach Harris. "I like to see my running backs block for their teammates."

Harold just nodded to me, but I could see that he didn't like being tackled by a girl.

On the next play, Oscar was supposed to block for me, and I was supposed to sneak up behind him. I got so excited when I got the ball that I forgot the pattern and outran Oscar.

"Oscar!" shouted Coach Harris. "You looked like you were moving in slow motion. You missed your block. Do ten wind sprints up and down the sideline!" Oscar looked exhausted, but he didn't say anything about it being my fault. I raised my hand. Coach Harris ignored me.

"Excuse me," I shouted. Everyone stopped except Oscar, who was still doing his wind sprints.

"It wasn't Oscar's fault on that last play," I explained to Coach Harris. "It was mine. I missed my assignment, and it made him look bad."

"Your job is to learn your position," said Coach Harris.

"My job is to run these practices."

"But it was my fault," I said.

"What a surprise," Eric muttered.

"Everybody!" shouted Coach Harris. "Join Oscar in the wind sprints. No excuses."

We started to run up the sideline.

"I'm sorry, Oscar," I said. "I tried to explain."

"No explaining in football practices. No excuses," huffed Oscar.

"Okay," I said.

When we finished, Coach Harris gathered us around him. "Good workout, everybody! Our first game is two weeks from Thursday. The league needs to see consent forms from all the parents before we play. I need the forms signed and delivered to me as soon as possible. Monday is the cutoff day. Now, go take your showers."

When I peeled off the girdle under my pants in the locker room, I had a huge black-and-blue mark that went from my buttocks down to my thigh. I must have gotten it when I tackled Harold.

It was pretty spectacular. I guess I was playing football for real.

JUST CALM DOWN

BY SATURDAY MORNING, I WAS GOOD AND SORE, but the practices had gotten easier. A lot of the plays were familiar to me from Peewee football. My moves did come back, and I remembered more about the game each day.

Mom had left me a note saying that she had gone to the supermarket. I went outside and did some stretches. It was a beautiful September morning. The air had turned cooler, but not cold.

I did a dozen push-ups.

Mom turned into the driveway and got out of the car. "How about using those muscles to help me bring in the groceries," she said.

"You got it," I said. I flipped open the cargo door.

"Every time I see you doing a regular push-up, I'm amazed," said Mom. "I've been going to the gym ever since your dad left, and I still can't do a real push-up."

"Well, maybe you should play football," I said to her. I carried the groceries into the house.

The bags were overflowing with potatoes, mayonnaise,

eggs, celery, and bacon. Bacon is the secret ingredient in Mom's potato salad. According to her, everything tastes better with bacon. I have to say I agree.

"Are you making potato salad for all of Clarence?" I asked.

"You know Beef and Robie's Saturday night barbecues. They always have a crowd. I wanted to make enough."

"Do you want me to help you?" I asked her.

"That's the idea. I figure the best way to pass down the recipe to you is to practice it. I was hoping we could do it today before your dad comes. Then I'll bring it to the barbecue."

I wondered if it would bother Mom if I showed up with Dad and Serena. Mom looked at me as if she were reading my mind. "Beef asked me if it was all right if your dad, Serena, and Jason came. It's fine with me."

I could tell by my mom's chirpy voice that it wasn't really fine, but I let it go. I had learned that when Mom spoke in that kind of false cheeriness, it was like an armor that you couldn't get through.

"Now, let's fry up that bacon," she said. Mom doesn't believe in cooking in the microwave. As the smell of bacon began to permeate the house, Mom began to relax. She put on music. We boiled the potatoes and cut the celery.

She was in a much better mood when we finished. I remembered the consent form. I brought it out and smoothed it on the kitchen table.

"I need your John Hancock," I said.

Mom loves history, and I knew that John Hancock was the first guy who signed the Declaration of Independence.

He signed in big letters so the king of England wouldn't have any trouble reading his name.

Mom's hands were still greasy. "What's it for?" she asked.

"Football. You know I made the team. Well, I need you to sign the consent form before I can play in a game. The league requires it for all interschool games."

Mom cocked her eyebrow at me. "You made the team on Tuesday. Today is Saturday. Did it slip your mind all that time?"

"Kind of." I was fudging. "I know you're not that enthusiastic about my doing this."

"Well, I'm not as interested in your being a boundary breaker as I am in your not breaking any bones. But Beef wouldn't put you on the team if he didn't think you could do it."

She signed the form. "Thanks, Mom," I said, giving her a hug.

Minutes later the doorbell rang. I looked at my watch. I hadn't realized it was noon, time for Dad to pick me up. He sniffed the air and wrinkled his nose as if he smelled something rancid.

"You might want to put a fan on in here," he said.

"We just finished cooking," said Mom. "Cassie was helping me."

"We made Grandma's potato salad with bacon for Uncle Beef's barbecue," I said quickly.

"You know that Serena and I don't eat potato salad with bacon," said Dad. "And of course, neither of us eats barbecue anymore."

"I'm going, even if you and Serena don't," I said.

"I didn't say we aren't going," said Dad. "Serena and I will decide later."

Mom wiped her hands on her apron. "So what do you think about your daughter following in your footsteps?" she said.

"So far I don't see her becoming a vegetarian," said Dad.

"I wasn't talking about food. I just signed the consent form for football. I left space for your signature too."

"That was stupid," said Dad.

"Now, just a minute," said Mom.

There was nothing that Mom hated more than being called stupid by Dad.

"You should never have signed it without consulting me!" shouted Dad.

Mom glared at him. "There's room for your signature."

"It's ridiculous."

"That's hardly fair, Geoffrey," said Mom. "She's been practicing all week. And she's been doing fine. I assumed you knew she and Molly made the team."

"Of course I knew about Beef going through with his hare-brained scheme," said Dad. "But I never thought you'd go along with it, Marie."

"I respect your best friend. I think it's daring of Beef to put girls on the team, and I'm proud of Cassie and Molly for wanting to play."

Dad glared at both of us. "Cassie, we've got to go," he said.

I put the consent form in my backpack. I didn't want to

pick a fight with Dad in front of Mom. I had learned the hard way that when I did, it only made everything worse. It was much better to fight with Dad out of Mom's sight. I gave Mom a kiss. "It'll be okay, Mom," I whispered. "Thanks, and I'll see you at the barbecue later," I said a little louder.

"I told you," said Dad, "I'll check with Serena."

"That's about whether you and Serena go," I said through gritted teeth. "I'm going to the barbecue whether you do or not."

Dad started to open his mouth to protest.

"She is old enough to make up her own mind, you know," said Mom.

Dad took a deep breath. "About barbecues, yes. I'll talk to Cassie about the football thing. This is one subject I think you've got to trust me on."

Mom bit her lip. "Trust" was not a word Mom would ever believe from Dad's lips. Her arms were wrapped around her chest, holding herself tightly.

I started out the door. Then I ran back and hugged Mom again.

"Cassie," yelled Dad. "Serena's waiting!"

"Lord knows, we wouldn't want to keep the Queen of Tofu waiting," I whispered to Mom. "Bye."

When I got in Dad's car I slammed the door closed on the passenger side. "You were rude!" I snapped. "Wrinkling up your nose at the smell of bacon in the house, as if it disgusted you even to smell it."

"You and your mother know I don't eat meat anymore," said Dad.

"Mom's house isn't your house anymore. You have no right to make judgments about what Mom and I eat. She doesn't make comments about you and the Tofu Queen."

"Oh, and where did you get that name for Serena, if not from your mom?"

"Big surprise, Dad! I came up with it myself. Mom is always careful not to put Serena down in front of me."

"Oh, yeah, I'm sure," said Dad.

"And how dare you call Mom stupid. You know who's stupid? You! You are such a stupid jerk!"

Dad slammed on the brakes and pulled over.

"I don't want to drive while I'm angry. I taught you never to make me angry when I'm driving. How dare you call me a stupid jerk!"

"You called Mom stupid. Mom doesn't put you down. You wouldn't know because you can hardly say a polite word to her. You were the one who left and found someone new, and you still act like you're the injured party all the time. You're not a saint. You may have stopped drinking, but it doesn't make you perfect."

"I never said I was perfect. Just calm down," said Dad. He started the car.

I glared at him. I had heard him say those words to Mom. *Just calm down.* It only made Mom angrier. She had stopped loving Dad. I didn't have that option. He was my only dad.

13

LAVENDER IS YOUR COLOR

AFTER DAD PARKED IN HIS DRIVEWAY, I GOT MY backpack and trudged into the living room. Jason greeted me with a big hug. I lifted him up and buried my face in his belly. At least I still loved *him*. I gave him a belly kiss. He laughed.

"Hi, Cassie," said Serena.

"Hi," I said. My voice must have betrayed that I was still angry because Jason began to squirm in my arms. I let him down. He clung to my leg.

"Play with me!" he demanded. "Play?"

"Give me a minute," I said. "I want to call Molly." I was still upset, and I knew that Molly would calm me down.

"No! NOW!" shrieked Jason.

"No!" I said.

He stuck out his lower lip and began to cry. He slapped me on the thigh.

"Quit it!" I yelled at him.

Jason cried even louder. He ran to my dad. Dad picked him up. "Don't worry, sweetie," he said to Jason, kissing him.

"Cassie's just in a bad mood. Maybe it's that time of the month for her."

"Dad!" I shouted. "That's not cute."

"Cassie," said Serena, "you do seem as if you might be ovulating. You know, I get powerful mood swings."

I rolled my eyes. "I am not ovulating."

"Ovulating!" repeated Jason gleefully. I was sure he didn't have the slightest idea what it meant.

"Shut up, Jason!" I muttered.

"Please do not say 'shut up' to my son," said Dad.

"My son!" I repeated. "Notice how you call him 'my son.' He's my brother. My brother hit me, and he screamed in my ear. And he used the word 'ovulating.' That's some word to teach a toddler."

"Right now he is acting older than you are," said Dad.

"I think Cassie needs a time-out," suggested Serena.

"I'd be glad to take a time-out," I said. "But I don't have my own room in this house. I'll take it outside."

I could hear Jason crying as I left. I felt like crying too. I grabbed my music player and stomped out to the sidewalk. I started to run. I just wanted to get away from Dad's house. A time-out! That kind of language was for two-year-olds.

I hadn't run away since about the last time I had a real time-out!

I took the corner double-fast. Then I decided to take a shortcut through an empty lot. When I was little I wasn't allowed to run any diagonal paths through empty lots. For some reason my parents thought that right angles were safer than diagonals.

I didn't care anymore. I took the shortcut. Through my earphones, I thought I heard somebody shout my name. I ignored it. I didn't want to speak to anyone. The bushes had grown up really high over the summer, and the path was overgrown.

A hand grabbed my waistband. I turned, ready to fight!

Of all people, it was Serena. She was huffing and out of breath.

"I've been chasing you!" she said.

I turned down the music player. "Sorry. I had my earphones on."

"I wanted to tell you I was sorry. Perhaps I shouldn't have said that about a time-out. I saw Jason hit you. He really loves you, but he's got to learn he can't do that."

"It wasn't really his fault," I said. "I was in a bad mood when I came into the house. I think he picked up on my vibe. Is he okay?"

"Of course he is. Jason's moods change faster than I can change his diaper. Your dad takes his shrieking a little too seriously. Sometimes it's as if he doesn't remember what it was like when you were little."

"I did my share of shrieking," I admitted. I still do.

We began to circle the empty lot.

"Your dad is really upset that you want to play football," Serena said.

I sighed. "He's being silly," I said.

"Don't call him silly," warned Serena. "He hates that word. Think of synonyms, like inane, asinine, ridiculous. Asinine is one of my favorites. It means behaving or looking like the animal, an ass. Like the donkey. I recommend asinine when you're feeling very angry." She giggled. "Sometimes he worries that you don't think he loves you, but he does," she continued. "He really does."

I shook my head.

"What?" asked Serena. I didn't know how to tell her that Dad was sending her to do his dirty work, just the way he used to send Mom to talk to me about "emotional" stuff. All this talk about how much he loves me just reminded me of the speeches I had to listen to when Mom and Dad were getting divorced.

"I think it would help if you said you were sorry," said Serena.

"You weren't there at Mom's house, Serena," I reminded her. "I'm not sure I am sorry."

Serena couldn't say anything to that.

We walked back to the house together silently. Dad was on the front lawn with Jason. "Mommy!" shouted Jason, stretching out his hands wide. Serena gathered him up.

"Hi, Jason!" I said. He grinned at me and started to laugh. Little kids are so forgiving.

"I'm going into the kitchen to start the salad we're bringing to the barbecue," said Serena. She went inside.

Dad stood with his hands in his pockets. I looked at him. He cleared his throat.

"I've been thinking about why I got so angry at you," he said.

"Me too," I admitted.

"I can't let you play football just because you've got

some whim. It's because I love you," he said quietly.

I was angry all over again. He just didn't understand. "It is not a whim that is making me want to play," I said through gritted teeth.

"Of course it is," said Dad. "You've got some macho idea that it's going to be just like when you were younger and you were a star. Except I know what football's like, and it's not for girls your age. You and I were just tossing the football around, and you got a black eye. You nearly got a concussion during the tryout. . . ."

"I could get a concussion running into someone in track, even falling off my bike. Molly got one playing soccer. Her parents signed the consent form."

"Molly is a whole different case. There are penalties for roughing up the kicker. There are no penalties for tackling the running back. Running backs have to be tough. I know. I was a running back."

Serena came out onto the lawn carrying Jason. "I'm glad to see you two talking," she said.

I looked down. We were talking, but we weren't getting anywhere. I lifted my head. I needed to make one last try.

"Dad, Uncle Beef thinks I'm tough enough. You should at least talk to him and hear why he thinks I'm good for the team."

"You know, sweetheart, perhaps you should talk to him," said Serena. "I think you at least owe Cassie that. We'll see him at the barbecue. You can talk to him then."

I almost fainted! Twice in one day Serena had tried to come to my rescue.

Dad glared at both of us. Then his shoulders slumped. "I'll talk to Beef at the barbecue."

He took Jason from Serena.

"Cassie," asked Serena, "would you help me with the potato salad?"

I watched Dad take Jason to his slide. "Leave him be for a minute," whispered Serena. I knew she wasn't talking about Jason.

I went into the kitchen to help Serena. She had out half a dozen cookbooks. They were all opened to potato salad recipes. I figured Dad must have told her what Mom had made.

"First we have to boil the potatoes and peel them."

"I've heard you don't have to peel the potatoes," I said. "There's a lot of good nutrition in the peels." I didn't want to tell Serena that I had heard that from Mom.

"Yes, that's true," said Serena. "However, sometimes looks matter more than taste—for example, every once in a while, I wear high heels." I couldn't begin to see the connection between high heels and potato salad.

"Don't laugh," said Serena. "Your father likes women in high heels. You'll see in a year or so. Men just like the way women's legs look in high heels."

"I'm tall enough as it is," I said.

Serena just looked at me as if I didn't understand.

I finished peeling the potatoes. "What's next?" I asked, hoping to change the subject.

"Now we have to blanch the string beans," said Serena, "and then the beets."

Each food had to be in its own concentric circle on the platter, first red for the beets, then green for the string beans. Finally we had to make a tight circle of the potatoes with just their edges touching. It looked like a salad that you would see in a magazine but that you might not necessarily want to eat. It took up the whole bottom shelf of the refrigerator.

"Okay," said Serena. "Why don't you get changed for the picnic?"

I looked down at the purple shorts and big red shirt that I was wearing. "Uh, I think I *am* dressed," I said.

Serena looked at me. "It wouldn't hurt to change," she said.

My shorts were a little spotty. When I cook I tend to wipe my hands on whatever I'm wearing. I went into the living room where I kept my clothes. A shopping bag that hadn't been there before was on the couch.

"What's this?" I asked.

Serena and Dad peered in. Serena was grinning.

"That's for you," she said.

"It's not my birthday," I said.

"I was shopping for myself, and I saw something that just looked like you," said Serena.

I opened the bag. I pulled out an Indian-style shirt with embroidery down the front. It was pale lavender and made of a silky cotton material.

"Oh, that's lovely," said Dad, in a voice that didn't sound anything like my father.

"It's beautiful," I said. "But I think it's a little small." I held it up. The arm holes looked tiny.

"I think it'll fit you," said Serena. "Come into our bedroom and try it on."

Serena took me by the wrist. I knew there was no way to avoid trying on her present. In their bedroom, I took off my big T-shirt. I was wearing a sports bra. I put on the shirt. It felt tight stretched across my breasts and tight under my arms.

"Oh, Cassie," cooed Serena. "You should see how pretty you look in that."

I looked at myself in the mirror. The lavender and lace around the neckline made me look feminine.

"It's beautiful on you," said Serena. "Now, I've got to take a bath. Show it to your dad."

I went in the living room. "Serena was right," said Dad. "It's just your color."

I looked at myself in the mirror again. I had read in a magazine that redheads shouldn't wear pale colors, but instead of making my freckles look like blotches, the pale lavender cotton seemed to give my skin a translucent glow.

I kept the shirt on. And I changed my shorts.

BARBECUE BLUES

JASON WAS DRESSED IN HIS SPECIAL BUFFALO Bills toddler football shirt. We put him in his stroller. We were off to the barbecue. Serena had asked for some time to herself, and she was going to drive over with the salad.

The sky was just turning pink. Some of the colors reminded me of my shirt. As I walked, the soft, silky material moved with me. It felt so good. I realized I was walking with my shoulders straighter. I was looking forward to my friends seeing me.

We could smell the ribs cooking before we got to the Harrises'. Aunt Robie greeted us in the front yard with a big hug. "Hi, Cassie. Congratulations on making the team. Geoff, isn't she the prettiest football player you've ever seen?"

"She's not really a football player, Robie," said Dad. Aunt Robie ignored him. She was giving Jason a Beanie Baby. Aunt Robie always had toys in her pockets. I looked at what she had given Jason. It was a stuffed cockroach. Jason loves bugs. Serena hates them.

"It's a cockroach!" said Dad. He sounded shocked.

"A love bug," said Aunt Robie. "Cassie, honey, Oscar's in the kitchen getting the food out to the barbecue. He could use a hand."

I walked inside to help Oscar. Oscar had on an apron. He was taking a pan of ribs out of the oven. Aunt Robie pre-cooked the ribs before they went on the grill.

Oscar straightened up. "Careful. This is hot," he warned, as he set the pan down on the counter. He stared at me when he straightened up. "Uh, pretty shirt."

I was embarrassed. "It was a present from Serena," I said.

"It's pretty," Oscar repeated.

I held the door open for him as he carried the ribs out to the backyard. Mom was standing next to Uncle Beef at the grill, laughing. She was wearing shorts and a big white shirt that showed off her tan. She took the platter from Oscar. Then she noticed what I was wearing.

"What a pretty shirt!" she exclaimed. "Is it new?"

"Uh, it was a present from Serena," I said. I wasn't going to lie.

Mom was staring past me, over my shoulder. I turned to see what she was looking at. Serena had arrived. She was wearing very slim jeans and shoes with no backs. Her heels were making holes in the lawn. She was also wearing a shirt just like mine, except hers was in black. She was carrying the huge salad.

I took a deep breath. Serena should have told me that she'd bought one for herself. I didn't want to be in some stupid mother-daughter outfits with my stepmother.

Oscar looked at me and then at Serena. "You're wearing the same shirt," he said.

"Duh." I regretted the sarcasm as soon as it was out of me.

"You look prettier in it than she does," whispered Oscar, loyally.

"Thanks, but that's not the point."

"What's bothering you?" Oscar asked.

I shrugged my shoulders. Oscar didn't have divorced parents.

"What a beautiful salad!" Aunt Robie said to Serena. She took the salad from Serena and put it on the table.

"It doesn't have mayonnaise in it, so it won't spoil," said Serena.

Serena looked at Mom's potato salad. Dueling potato salads between a mother and a stepmother could turn into an ugly backyard scene.

Molly and Ella arrived just at that moment. They both came over to me. "That blouse is great!" said Molly.

I rolled my eyes. "A present from Serena," I whispered.

"Why are you making that face?" asked Ella.

"Serena and Cassie are dressed like mother and daughter," explained Oscar.

"Uh-oh, wicked stepmother tantrum coming on," teased Ella. I took a deep breath and tried to calm down.

"Hey!" came Uncle Beef's booming voice. "Where's my next platter of ribs?"

"I'd better get inside and bring out some more food," said Oscar.

Molly and Ella put their arms through mine. "I don't care who bought you that shirt," said Ella. "It looks great on you."

Serena and Dad were walking hand in hand over to the grill where Mom was still helping Uncle Beef. It was all just one big happy barbecue. Eric and Harold arrived together. They made a beeline for us.

"Hi, Cassie. Looking good," said Harold.

"Don't even start," I warned him. Harold looked embarrassed. "Sorry," I muttered. "Not your fault."

Luckily, I was saved from having to explain myself by Uncle Beef ringing his loud dinner bell.

"Dinner is ready!" he shouted. "Right before the season, I usually tell the boys on the team to dig in first, but we've got a new tradition. So Cassie and Molly, my first girls on the team, come on and dig in!"

Molly and I went forward. Uncle Beef grinned at Dad. "I can hardly wait to start designing some plays for her. I do believe she's even a tad faster than you were at that age."

Uncle Beef piled my plate high with ribs and did the same with Molly's. I caught Serena looking at me, trying to keep her face from showing disgust. I didn't care. I am a meat eater. I swear ribs are my favorite meal in the world. I was just about to rip into one when Dad stopped me.

"Careful of your new shirt," said Dad. He handed me a napkin. Then he turned and spoke to Uncle Beef. "I think the idea of writing plays for her is a little premature, Beef. I haven't signed the consent form."

"Uncle Beef," I interrupted, putting down my rib. "Mom

signed the consent form. I don't need both parents' signatures, do I?"

Uncle Beef hesitated. "Technically, we only require one signature because there are so many cases where folks are divorced and one isn't around. But this isn't one of those cases. I won't feel comfortable unless both your parents are on board with this. Geoff, let's not let it ruin the party."

"Fine," said Dad. "I'm more than happy to drop the subject as long as you realize my daughter is not going to play in any real football games. You can keep her around at practices for a mascot. But the other teams will be gunning for her."

"Mascot!" shouted Uncle Beef. He looked angry. And then I could see him shift gears. It was as if he knew that his anger wasn't going to get through. He put his arm around Dad's shoulder.

"Part of what made you a great running back was that you were stubborn. If you couldn't get it done one way, you'd find another way."

"And your point is?" asked Dad, still angry.

"The point is, my man, that you've still got the stubbornness in you, but can you still find another way to get the job done?"

"What are you? The Yoda of football coaches?" Dad said. Somehow the fact that he was so rarely sarcastic made this worse. They were like two prizefighters jabbing at each other.

I expected Uncle Beef to get angry right back. He kept his right hand on Dad's shoulder, and as I looked closely, he was gently kneading it.

Dad's body became less stiff under Uncle Beef's hand.

"Cassie should get this chance," said Uncle Beef quietly. "Yes, I know she's a track star, but track's an individual sport. Being on a football team will be great for her. If she's angry or upset at something that happens in a game, she'll have people to share it with. When she plays a team sport, even when she's not at her peak, she can still help. She can set a block. She can deceive the defense. Give her a chance to have that, Geoff."

Dad just shook his head. Serena came up and put her hand on Dad's forearm and led him over to where Jason was sleeping in his stroller. They sat down at one of the picnic tables.

I watched him go. Whatever talent my father had for changing directions had frozen up inside of him. It was as if he had made one big change—leaving Mom and me and stopping drinking. Then he had frozen solid like some big woolly mammoth.

I walked over to a table where Mom and Aunt Robie were sitting with Oscar, Molly, and Ella.

"What's wrong?" Aunt Robie asked.

"Even Uncle Beef can't convince Dad," I said to the group. "He won't sign the consent form."

Suddenly Mom turned and grabbed my hand. She pulled me over to where Dad had sat down next to Serena. "Excuse me, Serena," she said. "Geoff, let's go somewhere quiet with Cassie and talk this over."

"This isn't the time," said Dad.

"It is!" said Mom.

"Go on, honey," said Serena. "I'll be okay."

Dad sighed. I hated the fact that he needed Serena's permission before he would even talk to Mom and me.

Mom led us to an empty table in the far corner of the backyard. All around us people were laughing and talking and having a good time. Dad took the side of the table that let him look back into the party, so he could still see Serena. Mom sat to his right. I sat to his left.

"Cassie, you know I love you," Dad began, looking at me.

I couldn't take it anymore. "Ever since you and Mom got divorced, you both begin every sentence with 'You know I love you.' You don't have to keep saying it. You say it whenever you want me to do something. You always get to do everything you want to do. I don't."

Dad stared at me. "Cassie, that's not true!"

"Oh, yes it is. You wanted to leave home, and you did. You wanted another family, and you got one."

"Cassie, you're not being fair to your father," said Mom.

"Fair?" I yelled. "When has Dad been fair? What was fair about him leaving you for Serena?"

"Cassie," said Mom, "going over old history is not going to help you get what you want. Look, Geoff, I know you love Cassie. I also know that you're scared for her. Yes, it would be lovely if she picked something less dangerous than football to challenge us about. I have a feeling we're going to have to face things like this again and again."

"You really think she should do this?" asked Dad.

"Should is different. I think we have to trust Cassie and Beef and everybody around her. I think the way to take care of Cassie is to let her play football."

"Mom's right," I said. "I love football. And you need to understand that. You can't make the rules for me all the time."

Dad sighed. "All right. I can see I'm outnumbered. But promise me you'll quit if it gets too hard."

"I'm not a quitter, Dad," I said.

"Give me the consent form," said Dad.

I took it out of my back pocket.

He signed his name beneath Mom's signature.

FIRST GAME: WHO NEEDS PITY?

I LOVED OUR PRACTICES. THEY BECAME MY favorite part of the day, even though they were hard. The plays were more complicated than in Peewee, but I loved the complications. I didn't mind that I rarely was given the ball to carry. My job was to deceive the defense so they'd think I had the ball.

During our last practice before our first game, the cheerleaders were out practicing too. Coach Harris called a 24 trap for Eric. I pulled to the right. Harold was playing defense and he was aiming at Eric from an angle. I tackled him hard at the knees. He fell on me, landing on my hip and forearm.

I had stopped him cold!

"Cassie!" shouted Coach Harris. I expected him to congratulate me. I got up, refusing to rub my hip, even though it smarted.

"That was terrible!" shouted Coach Harris, as angry as I had ever seen him. "Your head was down on that tackle. Never, ever tackle with your head down. That's how you get hurt. Give me twenty push-ups. I want you to *think* while you're giving me those push-ups. The next time you tackle with your head down, it's forty."

I started to do my push-ups.

"So how are you liking tackle football now?" hissed Eric as he walked by, practically stepping on my hand.

"Hey," I snarled, "maybe the guys on the opposing team will give me grief, but you're supposed to be on my team!"

"Cassie!" shouted Coach Harris. "I told you to give me twenty push-ups." Eric just walked away. He didn't apologize. I gritted my teeth and did twenty perfect push-ups. I wouldn't give Eric the satisfaction of knowing my whole body ached.

In the locker room after practice, I peeled off my girdle and looked down at my hip. My old black-and-blue mark now had new colors added to it.

The cheerleaders had come in from the field.

"Wow!" said Miranda. "That's some bruise."

"It's not so bad," I said. I was embarrassed.

Ella stared at it. "It looks awful," she said.

"I wonder what's going to happen at the game tomorrow," said Miranda.

"We're going to win," I said.

"No, I mean, I wonder if we're going to be hassled because we've got girls playing," she said. "It's so embarrassing."

"No, it's not," argued Ella, sticking up for us, but I could just imagine how much they had been gossiping about it before.

Miranda sighed. "Ella won't let us say a thing about you playing football," she said. "She keeps saying it's perfectly normal—but I don't think it is."

She flounced off.

"Don't worry about her," said Ella.

"I'm not," I said.

"But just between us," whispered Ella, "aren't you two scared of what the other team will do to you?"

"Naw," said Molly confidently. "We'll eat them up."

I looked down at my bruises again. "Easy for you to say," I mumbled. "They can't rough you up."

Molly followed me into the shower. "You're not scared, are you?" she asked.

"A little," I admitted. "Aren't you sore at all?"

"My legs have never been so tired," said Molly. "But you know what? I love it."

"Of course you do," I said. "You're doing great."

"It's not just that," said Molly. "I've learned something playing with boys. It's a little different than when you play with girls. The boys focus for the moment, but then they relax. I think girls could learn a little about relaxing from boys. The work is hard, but I can do it. I'm glad you talked me into this."

"Thanks," I told her.

"Thank *you*," she said. She gave me a hug.

When we came back into the locker room, Ella was by herself. "Tell the truth. Aren't you scared about the first game?"

"Naw," said Molly. "I'll be so glad when it's finally

Thursday and we get to play for real. I'm tired of practicing."

I didn't answer. Just talking about the game gave me but-terflies. I felt as if a whole butterfly colony had taken resi-dence in my stomach.

On Thursday morning Mom showed me what she was planning to wear to the game. I almost threw up. Her friends had gotten her a bright red T-shirt with a picture of me in my uniform on the front and the words MY DAUGHTER'S A FOOTBALL PLAYER AND I'M PROUD! on the back. Then they had other T-shirts made up for themselves with the words MY BEST FRIEND'S DAUGHTER'S A FOOTBALL PLAYER AND I'M PROUD!

"Mom, please don't wear them to the first game," I begged her. "It's embarrassing. I might not do well at all."

"Sweetie, we're all just so proud of you for trying," said Mom.

I hate it when adults tell you that they're proud of you for trying. It's so lame. Nothing I could say could persuade my mom not to wear the T-shirt.

The school had a pep rally at the morning assembly. A rainbow of balloons on stage celebrated the team. The cheerleaders came out first. They formed a V and we had to run out in between them.

When Molly's name was announced there were cheers, but when my name was announced, the noise level was def-initely quieter. It was as if everybody knew that we needed a kicker. Molly belonged. But kids obviously had a lot more doubts about me.

I stood there, framed by balloons. Later Ella told me that I had the same guillotine look that I always get when I'm about to run at a track meet.

I was glad when the pep rally was over. I actually found going to classes a relief. Everyone in the halls was driving me crazy by asking if I was nervous. It was good to have to go over algebra equations; it stopped me from thinking about what was coming up.

By the time Molly and I got to the field for the pregame meeting, I was a nervous wreck. But when I looked around at my teammates, I saw they looked as bad as I did. Oscar looked as if he had just thrown up. Eric was so nervous, his right foot was jiggling.

"All right," said Coach Harris. "It's a beautiful western New York Thursday for a football game. It's sixty degrees and sunny. Who wouldn't want to play football on a day like this? We all know the game plan. We're going to rely on our running backs. And, running backs, whatever you do, if you get into the open field, don't stop."

Eric and I stared at each other. I couldn't help it. I raised my hand.

"Why would we do that?" I asked.

Eric snorted.

"Look," said Coach Harris, "sometimes when you kids get out there in the heat of the game, you see daylight and it just freezes you. I want you to remember, when you see daylight, run. All right, into the locker room and change." He looked up at Molly and me. "Uh, locker *rooms*. We'll all meet out on the field. But remember everybody—pee before you put on your uniform."

Molly giggled.

"That wasn't a joke," warned Coach Harris. "You can't believe how many football players have to pee in their pants."

"Yes, sir," said Molly.

In the girls' locker room, it was so quiet that it was eerie. The cheerleaders weren't changing yet. It was still an hour before the game. Molly inspected the new color of my hip bruise. A little psychedelic yellow had been added to the black and blue and green. Molly gasped.

"It looks worse than it feels," I said.

"I'm glad," she said. "Because it looks awful."

We both went into the lavatory and peed. I started to get dressed and then found that I had to pee again. So did Molly. It wasn't funny. I think we must have peed five times as we were getting dressed.

Molly helped me strap on my shoulder pads, then I helped her with hers. With almost two full weeks of practices in full uniform behind us, we were a lot more comfortable suiting up than on that first day. I tried on my helmet. The helmet felt huge on my head. Then I took the helmet off and shook out my hair. Molly took a deep breath.

"You ready?" she asked.

I nodded. I think we were both too nervous to talk. We walked out of the girls' locker room side by side; our shoulder pads made us so wide we could barely get through the door.

We ran out onto the field. The band was playing in the stands. The band was never there for the track meets. You couldn't miss Mom and her friends in the stands. To make matters worse, they got to the game early so they could sit in the front row.

I didn't see Dad.

The Winchell Middle School team was already out on the field doing their calisthenics. In their red and blue uniforms, they looked huge. Our own blue and white uniforms sparkled in the sun.

Brant and Eric led us in our own warm-ups. Then Brant, our captain, went out for the coin toss. We lost. The defense took the field. All of us on the offense went to sit on the bench. I sat on the end next to Eric. I could feel his knee jiggling nervously. Finally it was time for the offense to take the field. Except I wasn't called. Eric went in. He didn't score, but the other team did with a touchdown. We were losing 7–0.

Late in the second quarter, Coach Harris put me in for Eric. I bounded out to the huddle. I was the cleanest uniform on either side, but I was finally going to play.

"Okay, Cassie," said Brant. "Red dog number three! I'm going to hand off to you. Oscar will open a block up for you. Go get it! And remember, if you see daylight, keep running." He gave me a pat as we broke out of the huddle. I was scared I was going to pee in my pants, even after all that peeing.

As soon as I heard Brant's signal, I shoved myself forward. There was so much noise around me, and so many bodies that I could barely see. But I got my hands around the ball, and I made sure that I tucked it in tight. I kept taking quick little steps, but I wasn't going anywhere. I had ploughed right into Oscar's back, and he was being pushed around by the other team. I felt something big and huge pound on me, and then I wasn't going forward anymore. I was literally being lifted up by my knees and thrown to the ground by the lineman from the other team. I managed to fall on my side and curl into a fetal position, keeping the ball safe.

As the referee blew his whistle, the guy who tackled me pounded me on the hip, right on my black-and-blue spot. "Welcome to real football!" he sneered quietly, so the ref couldn't hear him. At least I hadn't fumbled.

"Are you all right, Cassie?" Oscar asked.

"Of course," I snapped. I ran back to the huddle.

"You took quite a hit," said Brant in the huddle.

"I'm fine!" I didn't want their pity.

On the very next play, I again got the ball tucked into my belly and started churning my feet forward. But once again Oscar missed his block. The defender just tossed him aside and landed on me from a full jump.

I kept my hands on the ball, but his weight threw me backward. I could feel his hands groping for the ball. Then suddenly the football squirted out of my arms. I jumped up to try to dive for it, but I accidentally kicked it, sending it backward. I ran desperately after it, and I threw myself on the ball. I recovered the fumble, but we had lost twenty yards on the third down. We had to punt the ball away. The whole offensive team went back to the bench.

Winchell moved down the field with a methodical precision that made them seem more like a locomotive than a rival football team. They made an easy touchdown and had a 14–0 lead.

I sat on the bench, my eyes staring straight ahead. Molly sat next to me. None of the boys would sit near us, as if we had become bad luck omens.

"Maybe we'll come back," she said.

"I don't think so," I said. I was right. We never scored. We lost the game, 17–0. It was awful to have to watch the Winchell team fall on one another like puppies as they celebrated and rolled around on our field. They had won the first game of the season, and we had lost.

Coach Harris gathered us around him. "I want you to watch that celebration. It should hurt to see others celebrate on your field. I want you to watch and let the hurt seep in so we never have to see that again."

He sounded angry. I was too. I *hated* losing on our own field. I never wanted to watch another celebration like that again.

Eric bumped me as we walked off the field. "Welcome to real football, Cassie."

"Hey," I shouted, grabbing him by his pads. "The guy from Winchell said that to me, and I had to take it from him. But I don't have to take it from you. We're on the same team!"

"You booted the few plays that Coach Harris put you in for," Eric sneered.

"Look," I said, "I'm going to make it my job to be sure that nobody ever celebrates on our field again."

He laughed at me. "Oh yeah, sure. What makes you a leader on this team?"

I knew I was going to have to earn some respect. Eric wasn't just going to give it to me. Neither was anybody else.

When I got to the sidelines, I felt a hand on my arm. It was Dad. I had been concentrating so hard on the game that I hadn't even noticed when he arrived. I blinked. I couldn't believe that for the whole game, I had forgotten my parents.

"You took a pounding on those plays you were in for, but I was glad to see you kept your feet moving," he said. "You'll get better."

"I can't get worse," I told him.

"Look, don't take one loss too seriously."

I was still mad. "Dad, did you ever say that to yourself after you lost a game?"

"No," Dad admitted. "In fact, I guess I'm glad you're mad. But I still worry about you."

"If I don't start playing better, you'll have nothing to worry about," I snapped at him. "I won't get to play."

"And is that such a bad thing?" Dad asked.

I glared at him.

GIVE PEAS A CHANCE

ON FRIDAY NIGHT, WHEN I FINISHED MY HOME-
work, I sat down on the couch next to Mom to watch some
TV. I was wearing shorts. I winced as I sat. Mom looked at
me. The bruise on my hip had a whole new outline. It now
looked a lot like Australia.

"What's wrong?" Mom asked.

"It's just a bruise," I said. "It's nothing."

"Let me see," Mom insisted. I knew she wouldn't let it go.
I pulled down my shorts and showed her the bruise around
my hipbone.

It had turned an even deeper blue-black. Mom went to
the freezer and brought out a bag of frozen peas. "Here," she
said. "It'll help keep the swelling down. I think it looks
worse than it is. If you had to fall, that's a good fleshy part
of the body to fall on. You'll be okay."

"Thanks, Mom," I said, a little surprised that she wasn't
making a bigger fuss.

"Your grandmother used to keep her freezer full of

frozen peas for all your dad's football injuries in junior high and high school."

I lay down on the couch, and Mom put the peas on my hip. "It feels good," I said.

"The tiny little ones are best," said Mom. "They mold to the shape of your body. I used to bring frozen peas to your dad at the games. I'd keep them in a cooler for him."

"Mom, does my playing football bring back too many painful memories? I mean, like when you and Dad started going together?"

"Whatever happened between your dad and me, it was so long ago," said Mom.

During a commercial, Mom brought out a fresh packet of frozen peas and put it on my bruise. "You concentrate on the football; don't worry about your dad or me."

"I hated losing the game," I said. "I hated not playing."

"That sounds like your dad," said Mom.

"I used to think that you hated things about me that reminded you of Dad."

"That's not true," said Mom. "I never wanted you to feel that way. We both love you."

"When you first got divorced, you and Dad both said things like that all the time, but it was hard to believe."

Mom sighed. "We wanted you to do anything that would make you feel all right, but I guess we didn't realize that you would see through us when we were being fake. But it honestly is better now. I like the things in you that remind me of your dad. He's a good man. I actually think he's gotten better, and not just because he stopped drinking. I think he's grown up."

"Do you wish you were still married to him?" I asked her.

Mom shook her head. "I don't," she said. She smiled at me. "You look exhausted. Why don't you go up to bed? I'll bring you a fresh pack of peas. You can be the princess and the peas."

"Give peas a chance," I said to her, heading upstairs.

The next thing I remember, Mom was shaking me awake.

I groaned as I rolled over on my sore hip. "What time is it?" I mumbled. It felt as if I had just gone to sleep.

"It's nearly ten in the morning," said Mom. "Your dad will be here to pick you up in half an hour. Come on, honey, take a quick shower. I've got breakfast for you."

"Peas?" I asked her.

"A pea omelet," teased Mom. When I got downstairs, Mom gave me a cheese and peas omelet. She hadn't been kidding. Then she put two packs of frozen peas in my back-pack. "For the road," she said. She gave me a kiss.

"How's she feeling?" Dad asked Mom when he came to the door.

"She's pretty sore, but she'll live," said Mom. "They really piled on her."

"It's football. They're supposed to pile on," I said.

"Look who's lecturing us about football now," Dad said to Mom. "Young lady, your mom had to watch more football games and knows more about the game than almost any-body in this town."

Mom laughed. Who knew that my being a lousy football

player would get my parents to laugh together? And actually compliment each other. Life couldn't get much more weird.

When I got to Dad's house, Jason was taking his nap. I went to the kitchen to store the peas in the freezer. Serena stared at me. "You didn't have to bring vegetables," she said. "I've got asparagus. I thought it was your favorite."

I hiked up my shorts and showed Serena my bruise. "Believe it or not, it's looking better than it did," I said with a laugh.

Serena was still staring at my bruise. I had to admit that it had turned a particularly nauseating black, green, blue, and yellow.

"What would have happened if it was your face?" she asked in a horrified voice. "Cassie, you're just entering puberty."

"Serena," I said, "this bruise has nothing to do with puberty. And I'm not ovulating."

Serena was frowning. "Are you making fun of me?" she asked suspiciously.

How could I answer her without cracking up? "I'm sorry," I said. "It's just that puberty is one of my least favorite words. I didn't mean to make fun of you."

She didn't accept my apology.

"Geoffrey!" she shouted.

Dad came running. "What's wrong?"

"Look at the bruises on Cassie! She has a horrible black-and-blue mark on her hip."

"Mom saw the bruises," I said quickly, "and she didn't

freak out. You came to the game. You didn't freak out."

Dad looked from Serena to me.

He sighed.

Serena looked at my father. "Geoff, I don't understand how you can let her play such a dangerous game."

"He signed the consent form," I said. "He can't stop me from playing."

"He can withdraw it," said Serena. "It would be for your own good."

"Maybe Serena's right," said Dad. "Maybe you shouldn't be playing football."

He was making me furious. "I can't believe you!" I yelled at him. I threw the peas at him. He caught them with a shocked look on his face.

"That's just like you," I shouted at him. "At my home, a minute ago, you seemed fine and relaxed about me playing football. Even after the game. You say one thing to Mom and me, and another when we're with Serena."

"Cassie, that's so unfair," said Serena.

"Serena," said Dad, "let me handle this."

"Perhaps you and your dad need some alone time," Serena said.

"Alone time" is Serena's phrase for "quality time." Along with "puberty" and "time-out," they are not my favorite words.

Serena turned and left the room.

"I'm calling Beef," Dad said to me quietly.

"Oh sure, always do what Serena tells you to do. But I warn you, I'm not quitting the team."

"Look, you and your mom pressured me into letting you play. But I've never felt easy about it. Let me at least talk to him."

Dad picked up the phone and called Uncle Beef. They spoke for a minute, and then to my great surprise, he started laughing. He hung up. He went to the freezer and handed me a package of frozen peas. "You can keep playing," he said.

"What did Uncle Beef say?" I asked. I couldn't believe that Dad had changed his mind. My father never changed his mind, except I guess about Mom and drinking and eating meat. I thought about it. Perhaps Dad changed his mind more than I realized. In fact, that's what I had just yelled at him about. I felt confused. I put the peas under my hip.

Dad looked a little sheepish. "He reminded me of something."

"What's that?" I asked.

Dad helped me adjust the peas around the bruise. "Beef and I used to have frozen peas taped to every part of our bodies. Our motto was 'give peas a chance.'"

"Mom told me. But was that enough to make you change your mind?"

"Beef also said that you're like a pit bull out there, and he meant that as a compliment. He said you're tenacious, and he loves that in you. He said you remind him of me when I played. He also said he'll take my head off if I withdraw my consent."

"And what did you say?" I asked.

"I told him I'd leave it up to you, even if it kills me. And that if your mom can stand to watch you play, so can I. I'll explain my decision to Serena."

"Thanks, Dad," I said. I felt the tension begin to leave my body. I started to laugh, almost hysterically.

"What's so funny?" Dad asked.

"You'll let me play; Mom will let me play. Serena will have to live with it. The only problem is that I stink. You saw me in the game. Molly's so much better than I am."

"Molly doesn't have as much to study," said Dad. "As a running back, there's so much to learn."

"I thought I'd be good at it, but I'm lousy," I said.

"No, you aren't. You just take after me."

"Oh right," I said. "You were great."

"Not at the beginning," said Dad. "I wasn't the most talented player. But I was stubborn. I refused to let my mistakes stop me. I think you're like me. Your mom's stubborn, too. You get it from both sides."

"It sounds like a curse," I said.

He went to the television cabinet and rifled through the drawers. He pulled out some videotapes. "Want to see?" he asked.

I hadn't watched tapes of Dad playing in a long time. It was strange seeing him in junior high wearing the blue and white Clarence Coyotes uniform. In one running play, where he had a whole open field in front of him, he veered the wrong way. The only opponent between him and the end zone not only caught him but made him fumble.

At the end of the game, the tape showed Dad with his helmet off. He was spitting out the mouthguard. Suddenly

Mom came into the picture. She took his saliva-gooey mouthguard in her hand, and she was grinning up at him.

"Oh my goodness," I said. "She's got all your yucky saliva in her hand."

Dad smiled. "We were both so young then."

"Were you too young? Is that why you got divorced?"

"I don't think it's ever just one thing," said Dad. "We just didn't make it."

I looked at the videotape again. They were just my age when they met. How weird to think that I might already know the person I was going to marry.

Dad put his arm around me. "You know, sweetheart, your mom and I are the only parents you're going to get. And we do both love you."

It was a line that Mom and Dad had been using ever since they got divorced. I hugged him back. I didn't remind him that he had told me that a hundred times. Maybe I was beginning to believe it.

FULL TUSH DOESN'T HELP

OUR SECOND GAME WAS AT LANCASTER MIDDLE
School across town. It's in the richest area of Clarence.
Some of the Buffalo Bills players even have homes there. A
fleet of school buses was waiting outside after school to
take us across town. One was for the team, but the rest were
for all the kids and parents who had signed up to go to the
game. My parents were going, but not on the school buses.
They were taking separate cars.

Molly had brought her headset.

"It's not a party we're going to," said Eric.

"Hey, leave her alone," said Oscar. "Lots of the guys play
music on the trip."

Molly put away her headset.

"Are you nervous?" she asked me.

I sighed. "I peed three times before we even got on the
bus," I told her.

When we got to Lancaster, the Lancaster cheerleaders
escorted us to the girls' locker room.

"You don't look so tough," one of the cheerleaders said

to us. "I thought you'd have bigger muscles."

One of them tried to feel my biceps. I flexed.

"I'm strong enough," I warned her.

She laughed.

"Our boys can beat a team with girls on it any day," she answered. "Come on," she said to the other cheerleaders. "Let's get out there. We'll see you girls on the losers' bench."

"Nice," muttered Molly as they left.

"You're being sarcastic, right?" I asked. "She was awful."

"No, I mean this place is nice," said Molly. She pointed to the bottles of shampoo in the showers and hand lotion on the counters by the mirrors. Molly wiped some of the lotion on her arms and legs. "We're going to cream them with their own cream!" she shouted.

I laughed. I put on some lotion and then slipped on my girdle with the pads. Then I felt a little sick to my stomach. I went to the toilet and threw up. I flushed and then took a paper towel and cleaned up around it.

"It stinks in there," I warned Molly as I left the stall.

"Good," said Molly. "Let those cheerleaders smell a little vomit when they come in at halftime and we're winning."

"I just hope I don't mess up again," I said to Molly.

"I don't think that's the right attitude," she said.

I nodded. We went out to join the team.

We won the coin toss. On the very first play, Eric went back to receive the punt and the ball popped out of his hands without anyone touching him. He went after it on his hands and knees, desperately trying to recover it just the way I had, but he couldn't get to it. A groan went up from our side as Lancaster scooped up the ball and ran it into the end zone for a score.

Eric came back to the bench, his eyes downcast and brooding. "I can't believe that!" he screamed at me, as if it were my fault. I kept my eyes straight ahead.

"We're playing like a bunch of little girls!" he muttered.

"Hey!" I yelled at him. "We're not playing like little girls. We're playing like a losing football team. And we can do better. So don't use that phrase around here."

"Oh, and you've been such a great help," said Eric sarcastically.

"I will be if I get the chance," I said to him. But I didn't. At the end of halftime, my uniform was as clean as it had ever been.

At halftime, Coach Harris gathered us around him. "Our whole season is in front of us," he said. "It's time for you to learn that when your back is against the wall, somehow you can get it done. I'm often asked what I look for in players. Well, I look for attention span. Can my players keep their minds in the game? That's what I need from each and every one of you. I don't want to see panic in your eyes. You're in a game where hard work will be rewarded. Do anything half tush—and you'll be rewarded half tush."

Molly raised her hand. "I don't know what 'half tush' is," she said.

"Yes you do!" shouted Coach Harris. "You know how to go full tush. And that's why I'm glad you're on my team. And that goes for each and every one of you. Go out and give me full tush!"

Coach Harris called my number for the first play after halftime. I jogged next to Oscar. "Do you know what full tush is?" I asked him.

"No," he admitted. "Not really."

On the very first play, Brant threw an interception. A big Lancaster lineman smothered the ball in his hands and lumbered down the field. I tried to tackle him, but he swatted me away and I landed on my tush.

"That's not what he meant by full tush!" muttered Eric as we watched Lancaster score.

Coach Harris kept me in the game, but he never called for me to carry the ball. And Brant could never get his rhythm. He threw two more interceptions and Eric fumbled twice.

We lost the game, 21–0. We had lost two shutouts in a row and it didn't look like we were going to get any better.

GRASSHOPPER

BY PRACTICE TIME ON MONDAY, THE WHOLE TEAM seemed to be nursing bruises. Eric's shoulder was hurting. Brant's knee was bothering him. We looked like a walking advertisement for frozen peas.

Brant lobbed a screen pass to me. I cut up the field. I outran Harold and suddenly I saw the daylight that Coach Harris had talked about. There was nobody and nothing in front of me. It felt so great to be running as fast as I could, and nobody could catch me.

And then it happened. Suddenly my cleats hit the grass wrong. I fell flat on my face. I had grass stains on my helmet.

I looked down at my feet. I couldn't believe they had betrayed me like that, in front of everybody.

Coach Harris blew his whistle. "Hey, Cassie," he said. "Did a grasshopper tackle you?"

At first I was angry, as if he were picking on me because I was a girl, making a joke at my expense. Then I realized it *was* funny.

"Yeah," I said. "A giant grasshopper, but he's on our turf—

so I told him on Thursday, he's got to tackle the guys from Robin Hill."

The whole team started to laugh. After that we loosened up. On one play, I came out of my three-point stance so fast that I just exploded past Oscar.

"That's the kind of speed I want to see from you!" Coach Harris shouted.

Finally it was game day again. Molly and I were in the girls' locker room. We could now put on our uniforms without feeling like we were trying to get into space suits without gravity to help us. We both had learned the most important lesson. Pee before you put on everything.

"Are you ready?" Molly asked when we were all dressed.

I shook my head. "I have to pee again," I said.

"It's just nerves," Molly said.

"Nerves or not . . . I have to go," I insisted.

Molly waited. She was tapping her foot nervously.

We ran onto the field. "Let's go! Full tush!" Molly and I yelled together. The boys stared at us and then picked up our chant! "Full tush!" we all shouted.

"Full tush!"

We won the coin toss to receive first. Coach Harris called for Eric and me to go in together, the way we had in the game with Lancaster. Coach Harris gathered us around him. "Cassie! I want you in there. I want you to put your whole tush into faking them out. Brant, you're going to throw to Eric."

We lined up for the first play of the game. I was directly behind Brant. He pretended to give me the ball. I held my arms in front of my chest and tucked down low. I put my heart and soul into looking like I had the ball. I had the entire left side of the opposing team's defense fooled. One player coming after me was a giant. He must have weighed about 170 pounds.

He wrapped his huge arms around my waist and pulled me down. He threw his upper-body weight on me, knocking the breath out of me so hard that a snot bubble gurgled out of my nostril.

I liked it when my snot landed on his hand. "Oh yuck!" he said. I wiggled my fingers, showing him that I didn't have the ball.

Meanwhile, above us, I heard a yell from my teammates. I got up and looked down the field. Eric had broken free, and there was nothing between him and the end zone! He scored!

I jumped up and ran down to greet him. "Way to go!" I screamed. Eric was grinning. He and Oscar bumped chests. I started to jump too, but Eric dodged me. I didn't care. For the first time since the season started, we were ahead in a game. Molly kicked the extra point.

And that's when the heavens opened up. It began to pour steadily. We got the ball back, and the coach kept me in. I was so psyched to be playing more than just one series. Brant threw the ball at Eric, and the Robin Hill nose guard jumped up and grabbed it from him. He ran the interception into the end zone. They had tied the game.

Right before the end of the half, we moved the ball close enough so that Molly could kick a field goal. For the first time when we gathered in the gym at halftime, we were ahead, 10-7. We all were drenched.

Coach Harris was as wet as any of us. Ben went around giving us all towels.

"Town ball!" shouted Coach Harris.

We stared at him.

"Town ball!" he shouted again. "Say it after me!"

"Town ball!" we shouted obediently, but we didn't have the slightest idea what he was talking about.

"Town ball was what football was called in the Middle Ages," said Coach Harris. "Everybody got into the act—women, men, and children—they all had one goal: to win. Well, that's what we're playing here. We're playing full tush town ball, and I want you to keep playing that way. Remember what it felt like to watch Winchell celebrate on our turf. You don't want to see Robin Hill get to do that. We've got to hold them one more half, and we'll be the ones to celebrate."

I wanted it more than anything.

We ran back out onto the field for the second half. The rain made it hard to do anything. We kept having to punt the ball away after three downs, but so did Robin Hill.

Finally with only a few minutes to go, Coach Harris called a play where once again I had to act as Eric's decoy.

I did my part, but Eric fumbled the ball. The Robin Hill tackler scooped up the ball and ran straight at me.

I tried to dive after him, throwing myself in his path, but he sidestepped me and then nobody could stop him. Just like that, they were ahead.

Coach Harris called a time-out. He put his hand on Eric's shoulder. "Forget about the past," he said. "Put it out of your mind." I knew that Eric was not going to be able to forget that he had fumbled—twice.

After their touchdown, Robin Hill kicked off to us. Harold ran the ball from the end zone out to our own twenty-five. Brant got us into a huddle. "Cassie's going to get the ball. Eric, you block for Cassie and take the fake. Just like she did for you."

"Why don't we just use the play that got us our first touchdown?" asked Eric.

"Because this is the play Coach wants us to run," said Brant.

As we broke from the huddle, Eric clapped me on the butt harder than necessary. "Don't drop the ball," he said, "the way I did."

"Hey," I said, grabbing his jersey, "you're a great running back, and so am I. You made a mistake. Forget it! We've got a game to win!"

"She's right!" growled Oscar as he went to the line of scrimmage. He bumped Eric. "And don't forget it."

I put everything else out of my mind and got into my three-point stance. Right in front of me was Oscar's big rear end. Brant held the ball, then he pivoted. I charged. The ball fell into my belly. I clapped my arms around it and started my feet chugging forward. Oscar managed to get me a block so I could see just a little slice of daylight.

My legs couldn't get traction in the mud, so I just kept making little choppy steps. I looked up. There was only one defender between me and the end zone. I tried to cut away from him, but, just like in the Powderpuff game, my left foot slipped in the mud. My knees almost touched the ground, but this time my legs were strong. I stayed upright. The defender was on top of me. He was low, crouched to tackle, his head up so he could see what I was going to do. I knew that, because of the mud, I could not cut to the right or the left.

There was only one decision to be made. If I was going to score, I had to somehow plow straight into him and keep going. I tucked the football into my left elbow, tight under my breasts, and, at the last moment, I stuck my right arm into the defender's chest.

He staggered, but he managed to grab me around the waist. I didn't go down, but neither did he. I kept my legs moving. My uniform was so slippery with mud that the defender started to slip. Suddenly I was free and chugging into the end zone.

The Coyotes swarmed around me. My helmet got knocked off. Harold was pounding me on my shoulder pads. Everyone was celebrating. I looked for Oscar. I would never have been able to score without him. Without Oscar's block at the very beginning of the run, I would never have made it.

I jumped into Oscar's arms like a monkey. We had worked together to get the touchdown. The rain was pouring down.

He swung me around. Then all of a sudden it turned awkward. We weren't just teammates who had worked together. For one brief second, we were girl and boy.

I was shocked. Oscar was the last person I expected to feel that way about. Luckily we didn't have to say anything. There were too many shouts all around us.

I grabbed my helmet and went to the sidelines. Coach Harris pounded me on the shoulder. "Great run, Cassie! Great block, Oscar! Great fake, Eric! And, Brant, great throw! In fact, everybody did their job. Come on, Molly. You've got to kick the extra point. We still have a game to win."

The screams from our bench when Molly made the kick were deafening. The whistle blew. We had finally won a game. Oscar grinned at me.

I glanced at the sidelines where Dad was standing in a yellow slicker, holding an umbrella over Serena and Jason. Mom was standing a little to the side under a separate umbrella. I ran up to them.

Dad kissed me. Coach Harris grinned at Dad. "I told you. She's got your moves."

"She's just too stubborn to go down," said Dad. He looked at Mom.

"Beef's right," Mom said. "She gets stubbornness from both of us."

"I just never thought of my daughter as a running back like me," said Dad.

"I'm not a running back like you," I told him. "I'm a girl. I'm a running back like me."

"I'm so proud of you!" he said. "Go on. Celebrate with your team!"

Molly and Harold were walking arm in arm. I ran to catch up to them. Then, somehow, Oscar and I got pushed